LA JEFA

PATRICK M. HARRIS

Edited by
Stan Porter of
Instructorials.com
And
Anthony Sills of
Professional Pen Copywriting
This book is a work of fiction. Names, characters, places, and incidents are either the
product of the author's imagination or are used fictitiously. Any resemblance to actual
persons living or dead is purely coincidental.

La Jefa

Cover Art by- Natural Records Studio
ISBN: 1516865065
ISBN 13: 9781516865062

BOOK DEDICATION

This is book is dedicated to the Dreamers… Dream Big!
"Either write something worth reading about or do something worth
writing about."- Benjamin Franklin

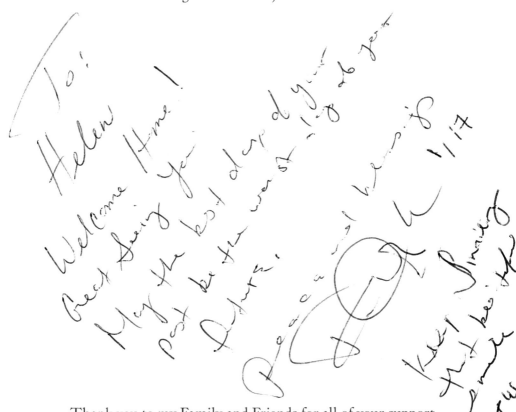

Thank you to my Family and Friends for all of your support.

Chapter 1

THE PLAN

Ring... Ring...

"Hello?"

"Yo, what's up my dude?" Erick says with a tired, raspy voice. "What's been going on playboy?"

"Shit, chillin' really. Not much," Zack replied. "Sitting here working on this project as usual. What's going on with you?"

"The same really... Tired and need a break from the everyday grind of this 9 to 5. You know we aren't meant for this shit."

They share a laugh.

"Dude, I really need a vacation," Erick continues.

"What? Who you telling? Really, I was thinking the same damn thing. What did you have in mind?"

"I said to myself, let me call Z and see what his schedule is like for the next few months."

Erick and Zackary have been best friends since the first day they met at Morehouse College in Atlanta, Georgia. They were both freshman, starting a new adventure, and all of it in a new city. Over the years, Zack and Erick have had some great times together. They have had stories and misadventures that would take days to tell. These two have been ride or die along the way, rarely keeping anything from one another, and have always been there for each other; whether it is advice about women or how to achieve financial independence. They love to see each other succeed in life. Although they live in two different cities (which may be a good thing), they still find time to talk every week and go on a few trips each year.

Theirs is a friendship that is that rare bond when two people just get along. When people first meet Erick and Zack they often say, *"How in the world are you two friends?"* But somehow, some way, it just works.

Erick is the more outgoing of the two. He has more street-smarts, whereas Zack is more analytical. Erick is definitely the risk-taker, smooth-talker, and he's not afraid to get shot down at the bar or fly by the seat of his pants.

Erick might cuss you out in a heartbeat, while Zack has always been dubbed the quiet sweetheart of the two. He uses his reserved, shy and calm demeanor to his advantage. He's got dimples women swoon over. He is also the cool and laid back one, while Erick is the life of the party.

They were nicknamed by their mutual friends, Easy and Trouble. See, that's the thing about these two. One would never guess that Erick is more sensitive and a very private person, and Zack is truly a party animal. They epitomize the saying that opposites attract. Where there is a Yin, there has to be a Yang. Where there is Erick, there has to be Zack.

Now in their early 30s, these two have been quite successful in their work and social lives. After graduating from college, they began their individual journeys in the corporate world. Now at the top of their respective companies, both have made wise business choices outside of their 9 to 5 jobs and started a few companies; even investing in real estate. They make sure to consult with each other in all aspects in life, whether it is work-related or social.

People often ask if they are brothers or cousins when they are together. Erick stands about 6 feet tall and weighs about 250 pounds. Zack's a little shorter at 5'10 and about 200 pounds. Both are brown skin, well groomed, handsome young men, and there is definitely no shortage of women that are interested for either.

The problem is they both refuse to settle. Marriage, may be one day down the line, but right now the duo's motto is *Work hard to play hard.*

When it's time to work, they get it done, but when it's time to play they play very hard. They really only work to travel!

"Dude this 9 to 5 shit is killing me, sitting in this office all day, and staring at a computer screen. This can't be the life. I wish I could just retire...like, yesterday. I want to sleep until noon, have my money make money and travel the world. Speaking of traveling the world, I really need this vacation."

"Mmm hmmm," Zack chimes in from the other end of the phone line.

"Z, I really want to go back to Brazil, but since the dollar has been tanking and the Brazilian economy has been improving over the last couple of years, especially since they just had the World Cup and about to get the Olympics, there is no way I am spending all that money to go back. Plus, we've been four times already. I think it is time for somewhere new. Awe the memories though."

"Yes the memories." Zack burst out with a song version "Memories" reminiscing, "What good times we had. So where should we go?"

"This guy at the bar was telling me he just got back from the Dominican Republic. He said if we liked Brazil, then this is definitely a place that we want to go check out. He said him and his boys chilled all day and partied all night. He mentioned that the scenery is to die for... blue skies and water, sandy beaches, hot weather, hot women, and lots of cold beer. The kicker is, he said, it's waaaay cheaper than Brazil. The Peso-to-Dollar exchange rate is like 43 to 1."

"For Real?" Zack says in disbelief.

Erick knew he was intrigued just by the way he said "For Real?"

"Yeah, I've been looking at flights around your birthday in June, and tickets are around $500. That sure sounds better than that $1300 each we would spend to go back to Brazil. Added bonus, the flight is way shorter too! And only one stop in Miami. The guy also recommended a nice place to stay called the *Vista Garden Resorts*, where rooms with taxes and breakfast included, run $49 a night."

"What?" Zack said astonished. "Only $49 a night? That's less than $1000 for the entire week trip. Alright let's do it!"

Erick started "dancing" and singing in his chair at work, "Time for new stamps on the passport! Dominican Republic, get ready!"

———

What had seemed like years, but really only three months, passed. It was finally the week of the trip, and both Erick and Zack were excited. The research had definitely been conducted as to what Dominican Republic had to offer. They even brushed up on the little Spanish they knew. They discussed the budget, which outdoor adventures and excursions they were going to partake in, what would be their first move, and even coordinated what they were taking with them. Erick always packs well in advance, while Zack is the more of a last-minute type of guy. Erick always gets a kick out of how Zack does laundry the night before, and then hastily throws stuff in his bag.

Finally, travel day had arrived. The plan was to meet in Miami since Erick lived in DC and Zack lived in Pittsburgh. Erick arrived in Miami for the connecting flight to the Dominican Republic. He looked around at the crowd by the connecting gate, but he didn't see Zack.

The flight was to board in fifteen minutes. Both of their flights were to arrive in Miami within a half hour of the other. Erick checked the *Arrivals* board. Zack's flight landed a half hour ago.

Did he miss his flight? Erick wondered to himself. Erick checked his phone for a voicemail or missed call.

"You have one new message" the phone said in a nasally woman's voice. The message was from Zack.

Erick expected Zack's voicemail to confirm what he hoped, that he was down at the other end of the terminal getting something to eat, but no such luck.

Instead, Zack reports that his flight is delayed. This wouldn't have been too much of a problem, but there were no other flights going to the Dominican Republic until the next day. Erick couldn't believe what he was hearing. Luckily, Zack had a friend who lived close by in Fort Lauderdale, so at least he had somewhere to stay when he got to Miami.

Erick boarded the plane to the DR not knowing what to expect. They had definitely not planned for this mishap, and now Erick had to travel to a new country without his Roadie. However, he was an experienced traveler and had traveled alone in the past, so he had no worries. At least this way, he could get a lay of the land ahead of time, and then when Zack arrived the following day, the fun could really begin.

I guess, Erick thought to himself, *I have a day to myself to walk around and get acclimated to the area*. He picked up his carry-on bag, pulled the ticket out of his pocket, and walked to Gate D 31.

CHAPTER 2

ARRIVAL

Bing Bong

The sound of the seatbelt alarm sounded loudly, and woke Erick up.

Bing Bong

"Please fasten your seatbelts. We will be landing soon" the stewardess said over the plane's PA system. Erick woke as the plane began to land. His first thought as the plane landed in the Dominican Republic was, *Yes, I'm finally here.*

He continued looking out of the window of the plane at the baggage handlers and airport staff. After he gathered his things, he gave his seat one final look, and deplaned. As soon as he crossed the threshold of the plane's front door, he could feel the heat from the DR blasting its' way through the airplane terminal. The heat and humidity was breath-taking. It had to be at least 95 degrees outside. *Damn why's it so hot? My goodness!*

After Erick grabbed his luggage, passed through the customs check-point, still enjoying the cool air conditioning from the airport terminal, he stared desperately at the automatic exit doors as they closed and opened. He dreaded going out into the heat.

Bravely, Erick stepped outside. "Ok first things first. I need a beer!" "It's hot as balls out here." Luckily, at this airport there are stands for that such thing. He headed toward one so he could sit back and formulate his plan.

His first step not only brought on the sweltering humidity of the DR, but an onslaught of harassment from the Porters, Taxicab drivers, and vendors.

"Sir, need help?" asked one man.

"Need a taxi?" offered another.

"Let me help you with your bags," piped a young porter boy.

"Would you like to buy Cigars or Souvenirs?" another said in synchronicity with the rest of the offers.

Erick felt a little uneasy with all the unwelcomed attention, sat on a nearby bench in the shade, and finished his beer and observed his surroundings for the next few minutes. *Ok, what's the hustle here?*

He finished his beer and walked to the opposite end of the terminal, and away from all the hustle-and-bustle of the porters, arriving guests, and beggars. He found himself immediately outside of the airport doors where people were exiting taxis, collecting their baggage, and entering the airport for their departing flights.

This end of the terminal was calm and lacked the peddlers, drivers, and young boys offering their services and wares. There is someone always trying to make money on the side, and catch a quick fare. During all the commotion at the other end of the terminal, he had been approached by guys who had offered rides as high as $50 in U.S. dollars to a group and $30 to an individual travelers. Cash-in-hand, he offered the next driver who pulled up $20 to take him to his hotel. The driver looked astonished, but quickly looked around and accepted the offer without haggling.

Damn I should have offered him $10US, anyways as always, cash in hand always wins! Bet, off we go to the hotel.

As the taxi traveled along, Erick enjoyed the scenery; countryside, blue skies, dirt roads, and the small stores and the shacks that lined both sides of the avenue. As he looked down the hill, he saw a speed boat that seemed to be flying across the blue waters.

The smell of gasoline is almost suffocating, he thought, as motorbikes passed the taxi. *That, and this heat!*

———

As the cab pulled up to the hotel, the doorman approached the cab and collected Erick's baggage. While he waited for the desk attendant to get the keys to his room, he felt a soft tap on his shoulder. Erick looked behind him and was greeted by a beautiful Dominican woman who offered him a drink with an outstretched hand.

"Is she the bartender?" he asked the front desk attendant.

He grabbed the glass, took a sip of the drink, and was pleasantly surprised how good it tasted. Not only was the drink good, but he couldn't stop smiling at the bartender. *She is fine; Halle Berry fine.*

The woman was a beautiful Dominican, 5'0, maybe 130 pounds, a slim but curvy figure, had long black hair, and beautiful brown sun-kissed skin. He handed her the empty glass. She smiled and told him to come see her at the bar later for happy hour.

I believe I am going to like it here. He started singing a T-Pain song, "I'm In Love with the Bartender!" He chuckled to himself. From the first five minutes of his visit, he could already tell this wasn't going to be the last time he fell in love. If the bartender was that pretty, he couldn't wait to see what the other woman in town were going to look like.

Yep, he was in trouble already.

After getting settled in his room, Erick decided to go for a little walk around to get the lay of the land. As he walked out the hotel, he heard someone say from a distance, "Hey there... what's up?"

Erick thought nothing of it since nobody there knew him, so he decided to ignore the call and kept walking. Out of his peripheral, he could see someone walking up on him fast and again heard, "Hey what's up?"

Erick turned to see a dark-skinned Dominican fella wearing a Yankees hat, white t-shirt, and blue jean shorts coming toward him from up the street.

"Oh, you talking to me?" Erick replied.

"Hey man, what's up?" The guy says using his best English. You could tell that Spanish was his first language, but he spoke very good *broken*

English. As he continued to talk, Erick's first instinct was to step back and clench his fist. As the guy approached and got closer, he was making friendly gestures; waving and such.

What the hell is he so excited for? Erick thought to himself.

The guy introduced himself as Yosi, and asked for Erick's name and which way he was headed.

Clearly I am walking down the street, he thought to himself. Since Erick was always a little skeptical when he met strangers abroad, he gave him short round-about answers.

"Erick, and I'm just out for a little walk. Just down here."

Yosi persisted. "My man, what's up? Where are you from? Did you just get here?"

What's up with the million fucking questions? Erick thinks to himself.

Erick turned and continued on his way to explore the town, and Yosi walked right alongside him just jibber-jabbering away.

"So I'm originally from the Dominican Republic, but used to live in New York. I miss Brooklyn. Do you know? I have a daughter there now. I came home to take care of my family, and never had the chance to go back. It is hard to get a visa. You kind of look like you could be Dominican, like we could be cousins. Where are you from? Is it your first time here in the Dominican Republic? You speak any Spanish?

"Un poco Espanola, Mi casa Washington DC", Erick said in his *just-as-broken* Spanish.

"Awe! Washington DC", Yosi said with amazement. "I have a buddy that drives a Taxi in Washington DC. I have never been to Washington DC, but I have a few friends that come to Dominican Republic on a regular basis from there. A lot of fellas come down here just to get away from the United States. You're going to love it here. You here alone? I can show you around If you like. I'm done working for today."

More than a couple of blocks from the hotel, and no real destination in mind, Erick agreed to let Yosi show him around town.

Erick giggled to himself. He then proceeded to hold a conversation with himself:

Hey why not? Yosi seems harmless enough; he just talks too damn much. I can deal with that. Plus it's always good to walk with someone… it's the middle of the day, with busy streets. Don't be a dummy and walk down any alleys and stick to the main roads of course. Momma ain't raise no fool! Anyways if he tried something I could probably take him.

The more they walked, the more Yosi talked. Yosi showed Erick where the best restaurants were, and of course his favorites, where the better liquor store was, and the best place to buy souvenirs. Erick just smirked and nodded most of the time. At some point, Yosi's voice seemed to become background noise as Erick's mind began to wander off, making mental notes of street signs, stores, restaurant and bars he might want to check out later on in the trip.

One thing Erick noticed as they walked through town is that Yosi knew EVERYONE. Everyone, they passed on the street knew him or he said *hi* too. He said *hi* to the street vendors, guys passing on mopeds, store owners, and the kids selling candy and gum.

As they walked and talked to people Yosi would say "Hey this is my friend from Washington DC, he came to visit me. I am just showing him around." One time, he even introduced Erick as his brother, and another time as his cousin. Erick laughed every time he said it. He was sure to let them all know that he was *his* guy.

Yosi made sure he introduced Erick to every woman they passed too. There were some that were just *alright*, but then there were some that looked like they belonged on a video shoot or on a magazine cover. Erick met some of the most beautiful women in town in the matter of minutes thanks to his chance encounter with Yosi.

Thinking about it, made him just shake his head. Another thing Erick noticed was that everyone had a hustle, so he was kind of wondering what Yosi had up his sleeve too. He thought he had it figured out; *show him around, and he will buy me some beers some food.* That sort of thing.

"Hey do you want me to show you how to get to the beach? It's only a few more minutes' walk from here," Yosi asked. "Just remember this road; it will take you straight there."

Since it was a Thursday, and the middle of the day, the beach was actually kind of busy. Filled with souvenir shops, beach shacks to get food and drinks, Erick even saw a stand where you can get a manicure, pedicure, and massage.

That's pretty dope. You can sit and look at the water while someone does your nails, gives you a massage, and brings you food and drinks. I don't know what heaven looks like, but I would imagine that it looked something like this. Erick thought the women in the scantily clad bikinis weren't bad on the eyes either.

After taking such a long walk, Erick got kind of thirsty.

Sure cold water would be ideal right now, but its vacation. Yep, time for a beer!

"Yosi man, I've seen the beach and the water, let's walk back the other way towards those restaurants you showed me earlier, and let's go grab a beer somewhere."

"Awe, I know just the spot, plenty of cold beer." Yosi grinned and hailed for a taxi cab to pick them up.

Erick thought as he watched the cab pull up: *What did Yosi have up his sleeve now? He seems full of surprises.*

After about a ten minute ride to the other side of town, they pulled up to what on the outside appeared to be a hotel. There was one man standing outside that Yosi greeted and told that they were there for a few drinks. Erick looked up and to his amazement, he was at a local strip club.

He smirked and thought, *Yosi, my man! The strip club... OMG (oh my god) I'm in heaven. Winner, winner, chicken dinner! You must have been reading my mind.*

"Okay, but let's not stay too long since I just got here," Erick conceded. "I do want to go back and get some rest."

"Okay, no problem. We'll only stay as long as you want," said Yosi.

Erick's mouth fell wide open, and his eyes got big as they walked into this club in the middle of the day...on a Thursday. The strip club was arranged in two areas. The first large room was like a lounge area with plush couches and fluffy pillows, and in the back there was a beach paradise set up with bar, beach chairs, umbrellas and even a pool. There were some of the most beautiful women that he had ever seen in this club, and he had been all over the world. All of the women were dressed in their finest swimwear and immediately flocked about and tried to get his attention.

"Papi would you like to dance with me? Papi do you want to go for a swim?" Papi this, Papi that. Heaven couldn't be this good.

Erick was focused on just getting to the bar, and tried not to give any one woman too much eye contact at one time. He felt as if he was developing a sore neck from whipping his head back and forth as the beauties walked by. Erick found the experience a little overwhelming, but the expression on his face showed that he absolutely loved the attention.

"Dos Presidente Curvesas Por Favor" Erick ordered from the bartender.

"Salute Yosi" They knocked beers with a loud *clink*! "Thanks for bringing me here. This place is amazing." Before Erick could say another word time seemed to stand still.

It was as if he had been thrown into a movie. The room slowed, both time and motion, a woman walked by with her hair blowing in the wind, the sun only shone on her, and a seductive song played as she walked past.

Boom Chicka –ah ow, Boom Chicka- ah- ow, wow! Oooooh yeah!

Erick was having that very moment. He heard Yosi saying something, but his focus was completely on the light-skinned, blondish brown hair, 5'5" with the knockout-body with tattoos, as she gracefully glided towards the bar and took a seat right beside him. She extended her hand.

"Hola Papi."

"Hola cómo estás?"

"Bien, y tu?"

"Bien Cómo se llama?"

"Erick" y tu?

"Angel."

"Angel, Nice to meet you, ummm Mucho Gusto", Erick rattled off in his Spanish that now seemed to be too little at this point. He thought to himself, *Lawd her name is even Angel!*

Luckily, he had Yosi there to help him translate. He had proved useful after all. Erick told her they had just stopped in for a drink. Yosi was showing him around and they had not planned to stay too long. After a few drinks, great conversation and scenery, Erick agreed to meet up with Angel later on that evening so she could show him around town, have dinner, and go dancing. They said their *goodbyes* and ended with one of those "good" long hugs.

Whew, glad I got out of there when I did. I can't wait to see her later. I need to go back to the hotel to rest up. Where the hell is Yosi's ass? Erick thought as he looked around.

Yosi's smiled and piped up, "Hey, I got another spot to show you before we head back. It's only up the road a little bit. If you like this spot you will definitely like this other spot."

"Pissh! Ain't nothing beating this spot Yosi!"

Erick would soon learn how wrong he was with this statement.

As soon as they stepped through the door, Erick spotted five guys sitting around two bars. The next thing he noticed were 30-- yes, 30 women--tall ones, short ones, thick ones, skinny ones, dark, brown, light, damn near white, all kinds of women.

Erick thought to himself, *Lord thank you for making all of these beautiful women. Amen. CHURCH!* Erick snapped a few pictures with his phone to send Zack. He knew without pictures… *Zack would never have believed this shit!*

Yosi and Erick found seats at the bar and decided to have a few more beers.

Before long, it was like sensory overload.

"Ok Yosi, enough with the tour. I can come back here later. Better yet, I'll just wait until Zack gets here. I just arrived and I'm already six beers in. I've been traveling all day. I need to hit the store for some snacks and drinks for my room, take a shower, and relax. I may even take a quick nap."

During the short walk back towards the hotel, Yosi was doing what he did best; jibber-jabbered the entire way. Erick thought about the Angel, the beauty he had left earlier at the first club, and he could not wait to see later. He braced himself for what he knew already was going to be a long night.

"Hey, Angel doesn't get off until 11:00 PM, do you want to go and watch the game?" Yosi asked.

"Oh hell yeah, the NBA playoffs, are they showing it somewhere close?" Erick inquired.

"Ok, I'll be back at 8:00 and we can go down to the sports bar which is a few blocks from where you need to meet Angel." Yosi promised.

"Cool, that will give me enough time to relax, take a nap and shower for tonight."

"Hasta Luego Erick."

"Hasta Luego Yosi."

Yosi and Erick parted ways near the hotel entrance.

The alarm clock display switched to exactly Eight o'clock, and Erick's hotel room phone rang out loudly.

"Hello?"

"Hola! Mr. Erick you have a visitor at the front desk," said the voice.

"Okay, I'll be right down."

Of course it was Yosi's ass, Erick thought, *Right on time.*

"Well, let the night begin!"

Relaxed, showered, and feeling like a new man, Erick was ready to take on the night. He met Yosi in front of the hotel, and they made quick time of the two blocks from the hotel down to the sports bar.

Erick's first priority was to get some food in his stomach, because he still planned to go out later that night with Angel. It was going to be a long night, so he wanted to coat his stomach properly before the drinks started flowing once again.

Ever since he landed in Dominican Republic he had been craving some authentic Dominican food; Arroz con Pollo (chicken and rice) to be exact. All he could think about while he was on the plane was sitting down with a cold beer and a nice big plate of Arroz con Pollo. Since Yosi was nice enough to show him around earlier, Erick offered to pay for his meal also.

After getting their food, Erick and Yosi found a table in the crowded sports bar. As they began to dig into their food, Erick looked around the bar and noticed that women were EVERYWHERE.

He thought. *The other two spots Yosi showed me were jumping, but damn, where did all these people come from?*

It seemed like as soon as the sun had gone down, everyone had come out of their houses. Everywhere he looked there was another beautiful woman.

"I know I must look like a fish out of water, because all the women are trying to get my attention."

After a second he realized fish and water have nothing to do with it. He knew exactly what he must look like to the local women- an American tourist with a pocket full of money. He chuckled to himself. He played it cool, ignoring advances from the women, especially since he was enjoying his food and watching the game.

He enjoyed just sitting and chatting with Yosi in between bites of the delicious food. Anyways, he knew once the game was over, it would be close to the time he was to meet up with Angel after her shift has ended.

As Erick and Yosi finished their meals, a female approached the table, smiled and said hello to Erick and Yosi; giving the latter a hug. She then asked if she could sit down.

"Sure, no problem," as both Erick and Yosi gestured for her to have a seat at the empty chair at their table.

Yosi introduced Erick as his friend from DC, and of course Erick had a good laugh to himself since they had just met earlier that day. One might have thought they were friends since they spent practically the whole day together. Erick thought, *I guess we are cool. Not exactly old friends, but we cool.*

There was something about the girl that Erick could not figure out. But, he definitely seemed to like it. She wasn't half dressed like most of the other females around who had been begging for his attention. She was a very attractive young lady, and had an unexplainable aura - a glow - about her. She seemed to be different; maybe it was the way she carried herself.

She didn't ask him or Yosi to order her drink, but instead took it upon herself to order the table another round, which Erick found a refreshing change of pace. There was something that Erick couldn't quite put his finger on, but he was intrigued.

She was about 5'5", maybe 135 pounds, with a nice caramel complexion, wavy brown shoulder-length natural hair, and beautiful hazel eyes. She didn't have on goo-gobs of makeup like most of the other women, and her natural beauty radiated in the little restaurant as a result. She wore a pair of nicely-fitted jeans that accented her curvy figure, and a low-cut pink top that framed her nice and perky breasts.

She introduced herself in Spanish and then English. She spoke English quite well, which came as a huge relief to Erick. He wouldn't be forced to communicate with his *broken* Spanish. This young beauty had his full attention.

Her name was Damani.

CHAPTER 3

LA JEFA

Damani was born in Santiago, Dominican Republic to Esteban and Consuela Cruz. She was her father's only child and her mother died while giving birth to her. Esteban never remarried and he never loved another woman like he did Consuela.

She grew up almost like any other child in the Dominican Republic. She was full of life, loved the beach, and the ocean. There were some differences between her family and those of her friends, but Damani was too young to notice. In fact, growing up she never questioned why her family was so well off. But from time to time, she would hear rumors about her father from her classmates.

On the day Damani turned thirteen years old, she confronted her father and demanded that she be told the truth. It was time to find out if the rumors were true. Esteban sat her down and asked her if she was truly ready to be a part of the Cruz Family. Damani was a daddy's girl and totally committed to her father. She said "yes" without a second thought. So, that night Esteban took his only daughter into the slums. He'd received information about a guy who was stealing money from the store the Cruz family owned.

Damani and Esteban pulled up to a vacant shack, and inside she was surprised to see that her Uncles Luis, Papo and Jorge, not really her blood Uncles, but Esteban's Captain and Lieutenants had a guy secured to a chair in the middle of the floor. The man vehemently denied taking money from Esteban and the Cruz family. Esteban got down on one knee and looked Damani straight in the eyes and said to her "Nobody ever steals from our family, disrespects our family, or lies to our family. We are family. Do you understand?" The frightened 13-year-old nodded in agreement to her father.

Esteban continued, "He took food out of your mouth and money out of your pockets. What are you going to do about it? He must be made an example of. " With his legs and arms bound still, Esteban kicked the man out of the chair and onto the floor. "Pick him up and put him on his knees" Esteban barked out his orders. They quickly obliged placing the man on his knees. In front of Damani, Esteban placed a gun and a knife on the chair where the man once sat. Damani picked up the gun but it was too heavy for her adolescent grip. She put it down and tentatively picked up the knife. She was so nervous her hands were shaking. Esteban and Damani's uncles' eyes were gleaming with anticipation. They waited silently to see what Damani would do next. With the blindfolded man on his knees continuing to deny taking any money from the Cruz family, Damani gripped the knife the way she'd seen the family's cooks do with the livestock many times. She found her place for the knife under the man's chin. With the knife in her right hand, Damani grabbed the man's head and yanked it back, exposing the man's throat. The man began to cry and continued to deny stealing money from Esteban. Before anyone could react, she quickly applied pressure and sliced the man's throat from right to left.

As the blood spurted from the man's severed neck, Damani stood frozen in place with no expression on her face. The man's lifeless head hung down and blood oozed from his throat down the front of his clothing. For a few minutes nobody spoke and nobody moved. Then, Esteban, seeing what the others could not, that his daughter was visibly shaken about what she had just done, took the bloody knife out of his daughter's hands.

"Do you understand why we do what we do?" he asked Damani. "Nobody comes between our family." Then he hugged his daughter tightly and welcomed her to the La Familia Cruz. His brothers in crime began to cheer and shoot their guns in the air in celebration. That was the night Damani's life changed forever.

She was no longer allowed to attend public schools with the other children. She was home-schooled by the best teachers in the Dominican Republic. She was taught to speak English, French, and Chinese. In the afternoons she was trained by former Dominican Republic military in combat and interrogation tactics. She caught on very quickly and adapted to her new curriculum.

———

Over the next two years, Damani was often called upon to make runs for the family and collect money people owed. Because of Esteban and her "uncles'" reputations, nobody dared cross Damani. The word quickly spread about El Commodore's no-nonsense daughter.

As she started to develop her own reputation, Damani quickly graduated from making runs for her father to helping him run his business. She became one of the youngest enforcers. Despite how incredulous it may sound, from age sixteen until she turned 21, Damani's reputation only grew more fearsome. The streets whispered about the female gangster that reported directly to El Commodore.

Esteban didn't trust many people but he knew he could always count on his daughter to get the job done. Nobody would speak of it openly, but there was a rumor that Damani had once tortured a man for ten hours straight, and then one by one, killed each of his family members until their bloodline was no longer in existence.

When Damani turned 21, she and Esteban stood side-by-side. You could say that she'd come a very long way from being the scared little girl with the shaky hands. By the time she reached 25, Damani's beautiful sun-kissed, caramel skin, long wavy brown hair and hazel eyes made her an undisputed beauty. She stood about 5'5" and weighed about 135 pounds.

Esteban still ran the show, but due to his declining health, he depended on his brothers and Damani more and more to help him run the operation. Even though her uncles' were older and had more experience, Damani was a quick study and quickly established herself as the brains of the operations. Of course she wasn't just brains. She had plenty of brute force at her disposal too. This lethal combination made the Cruz family a lot of money. Damani even boosted the organization's earning power by restructuring the day-to-day operations and investing the money wisely. Damani had come into her own. The townspeople have even given her a nickname...*La Jefa*.

CHAPTER 4
THE ROMANCE

Roars from the sports bar patrons erupted as the NBA playoff game was broadcast, the score very close, and only minutes left in the game; however, Erick's full attention was on Damani. Nothing else mattered to him at this time, but getting to know her better. As minutes turned into hours, they sat, laughed, drank and enjoyed each other's company.

Erick noticed the little things about her, like the way she adjusted her hair behind her ears, the way she touched his hand softly as she laughed, and her smile when she looked at him. Her hazel eyes appeared to sparkle as she gazed into his, as they conversed.

Snap out of it fool, you can't fall in love the first day. Erick was truly mesmerized, not only by her beauty, but by her conversation too. Another restaurant patron squeezed into a seat at the table directly behind Damani's seat; bumping her chair in the process. Erick quickly took the opportunity to pull her chair closer to him. She placed her hand on his thigh and said, "Thank you Papi," and gently kissed him on the cheek.

Her lips were soft like velvet rubbing on a baby's ass, he thought. Erick confused as why she kissed him suddenly said, "You are welcome and Thank you, but what was that for?"

"Just for being a gentleman," she said. She told him that she was enjoying herself, and explained she had been having an interesting day. Before she came to meet Erick, she had run into an old acquaintance that she hadn't seen for years. "It was really weird seeing him back in town after all this time" she said sort of under her breath, and then quickly changed the subject.

"I'm glad I came here. This is the highlight of my night," she said.

"Well, the night doesn't have to end," Erick said hoping she would take him up on the offer. "It's still early."

The strip was in full-party mode. The restaurants and bars were filling up with people. The sun went down, and people came out of the woodworks. He hadn't noticed the crowds.

The vampires and freaks must come out at night, Erick thought to himself and laughed. He was so engrossed in Damani; he forgot Yosi was still with them. Yosi saw an acquaintance, and then excused himself from the table. He walked down the street leaving Erick and Damani at the table. Erick called the waitress over and ordered another round of drinks, and Damani excused herself to "freshen up."

She had only left for a few brief moments, but in that time, a group of females saw Erick sitting there by himself, approached, talked and flirted with him. Upon seeing Damani return to the table, they politely said hello to her and quickly walked off.

The waitress arrived with the next round of drinks at the table. They raised their glasses and toasted to new friendship and a good night together.

There is nothing more refreshing than a cold Presidente beer on a warm night, Erick mused.

They looked at each other, and stared longingly into one another's eyes, moved closer and closer, and finally met for a singular kiss. Again, Erick was living a scene from a movie he had seen.

Erick swore when they kissed fireworks, bells, horns and sirens and whistles sounded. It could have just been the loud music, horns from the cars and motorcycles racing up and down the crowded street, but whatever it was, Erick knew one thing; *that kiss was amazing!*

Damani too, said she saw one of her friends and excused herself from the table. Once again, a group of females saw Erick sitting there by himself, and approached. He entertained the conversation for a brief moment, but it only took that long for Damani to walk back up to the table.

She threw her arms around Erick and kissed him on his cheek. Once again the other women said hello to her, apologized and quickly were on their way.

Erick sat back in his chair and just laughed. He began to notice once she was around that none of the other females bothered him. He jokingly started calling her his little protector. Damani said she was tired of the sports bar scene, and she wanted to show him more of the nightlife in the town. Erick quickly agreed, paid the tab, and they walked hand-in-hand down the street to another bar; her favorite. Of course, she knew the bartenders and all the staff. They greeted her with kisses, hugs, and handshakes, and after a brief introduction, greeted Erick with the same. Erick thought to himself, *they're very affectionate. The culture in the United States is totally different when meeting new people.* Damani and Erick took seats at the bar and continued their night.

The bar had beautiful bartenders serving strong drinks, Latin and hip-hop music blaring over the speakers, and beautiful women dancing everywhere around the crowded bar. There was a lot to take in. All Erick could think about was that when Zack arrived the next day, *this shit is about to get really crazy. I'll have my partner in crime with me and we can really cut up. Turn up time! This is off the hook.*

Erick pulled his camera out his pocket and took a few pictures of the "sights" in the crowded bar for those fellas who weren't able to come on the trip. Before he knew what had happened, Damani grabbed the camera, pulled him close, and started taking pictures of them together. He took the camera back, and snapped some pictures of her as she posed for him on the bar like they were in a private photo shoot.

Out of nowhere, Yosi (who they had forgotten about as soon as he left) showed up at the bar and saw Damani and Erick taking pictures. Of course, he grabbed the camera from Erick and he pretended to be their own private photographer as he took more pictures of Erick and Damani together.

Yosi was quite shocked to see them pose kissing for one of them. Erick and Damani had become pretty flirty at the bar; his hands on her thighs, her hands rubbing his arms, Damani dancing in front of Erick seductively while he sat in the chair as she looked back and smiled.

Erick thought to himself, *you keep bouncing that cute little ass between my legs, and you're gonna get a surprise you might not be ready for girl!*

As the night continued, the drinks kept flowing and Erick was introduced to more of Yosi and Damani's friends. One of the girls Damani had spoken to earlier approached and whispered something in Damani's ear. Erick laughed and was having a good time joking with Yosi. He did not see the concerned look on her face as she leaned over to him and excused herself from the bar.

"I'll be right back Papi, I need to go with her to take care of something, and I will be right back".

Erick was indifferent, and assumed that the way the night had been going, he had gotten use to her running off and coming back. Besides, there was good music playing, plenty of drinks, and a lot of sights to be seen. Yosi was quick to tell the other females at the bar while Damani was gone Erick was off limits. They didn't take heed of Yosi's warning and kept pushing up on Erick.

When Damani returned, the girls were astounded. They were rushed, stumbling, and quick to remove themselves from the area around Erick. Erick seemed puzzled. Why had Damani had such an effect on the other females? He was amused by the entire series of events.

With all this attention, he thought to himself, *shoot, if I keep Damani around it will keep me from getting harassed all night long*. Eventually, even Yosi got in on the joke. The idea seemed preposterous; this small female was protecting such a large man from all of these "unwanted attacks." Yosi and Damani both really looked out for Erick all night long and had made him feel welcome in this new place.

Erick had lost track of time, and it was now 2:00 a.m. The bar had started to dwindle down and Damani laid her head on Erick's shoulder looking up at him with her hazel eyes.

"Papi are you tired and ready to go?"

Erick looked over to ask Yosi if he was ready to go, but he had his head down on the bar.

"We will take that as a *yes*. Yosi is done and ready to go."

He agreed it was time to leave, however, he didn't want to leave Damani. It had really been a long day for Erick, and when Zack arrived he knew they would be doing it all over again. Erick shook Yosi, said they were leaving, and Yosi sat up. All three said their goodbyes to Yosi and Damani's friends at the bar and proceeded to walk up the street toward Erick's hotel.

"Damani do you want me to get you a taxi?"

She declined and asked, "Why? You so tired you want to catch a cab to the hotel?"

Erick laughed, "No, I thought you might want a cab home."

"No Papi, I'm not going home, I'm coming with you to the hotel for a beer."

As the three of them walked up the street—Erick had Yosi on his right and his little protector Damani on his left--talking and laughing all the way until they finally arrived on the cross street to the hotel. Erick and Damani bid Yosi a good night and vowed to meet up the next day when Zack arrived in town. Damani said her feet were hurting and reached down and took her shoes off in the middle of the street. Erick scooped her up, put her on his shoulders, and carried her like a boom box. She started laughing and screaming for him to put her down. Erick obliged, and unexpectedly she hopped on his back. He carried her on his back the short trip to the hotel.

———

The two entered Erick's room, Damani opened the fridge and took out a beer he had bought earlier that day. She poured herself a cup and handed him the rest of the bottle. They toasted to a good night, kissed, and then took a drink. She asked if he minded if she took a shower.

"Umm of course not"

He said he needed to take one too after being hot and sticky in the bar all night. A nice lukewarm shower seemed like it would definitely do the trick right now. Before Erick had a chance to realize what he had just agreed to, she was standing naked in his bathroom. She looked back at him, smirked, and hopped into the shower.

Erick closed the door behind her, and then hid his valuables. Although she seemed to be interested, Erick was concerned. He thought, *it doesn't matter, if somebody sees it, they will steal it.* The bathroom door opened, steam rolled out of the shower, and then out stepped a naked, and wet, Damani.

"Que Pasa? Vamanos Papi."

Erick quickly got undressed and joined her back in the shower. Erick had never been undressed that quickly before in his life. The water felt great. She began to slowly wash his body and he washed hers. He couldn't decide which felt better - the water or the warm touch of her hands – but knew the combination made for quite a show.

"Mmm, Papi", she said as her eyes got big. "Wow," as she glanced down.

Slowly, he ran his soapy hands down her back and cupped her buttocks. He began to kiss her neck and shoulders. She moaned as he ran his tongue down her breast and sucked her nipple. He turned her around and kissed the back of her neck and ran his tongue down her back. She backed her butt into him and began to grind slowly while he grabbed her breast and reached around and played with her clit. She turned off the water grabbed a towel and dried Erick off. He took the other towel and did the same to her. She ran to the bed, dropped the towel, and climbed in.

"Come on Papi, mucho frio."

Erick laughed, took a sip of beer and grabbed a condom off the table. For the next two hours they explored each other's bodies. Erick tried his best to break her, wanting her to give in and admit he was too much for her, but she stood her ground. As much as he gave, she gave him back.

Erick felt a glimmer of empathy for the neighbors because the wooden bed kept moving, scooting, and squeaking loudly along the tile floor; and then there was Damani's loud cries of passion.

He laughed to himself, and thought, *I just hope the neighbors are enjoying the show and getting some too!*

Finally, both exhausted, they laid naked on the bed, trying to regain their breath. Damani got up grabbed a sheet off the bed, wrapped herself in it and cracked open another beer.

"Papi does this door open" she asked as she pulled back the curtain to reveal a door leading to the patio outside the room. Erick got up to unlock the door. There was a nice warm breeze as they sat on the patio outside, the room was covered in bed sheets, and they drank beer and watched the sun rise. They finished their beers, tried to fix the bed as best they could, then collapsed together.

What a night! Erick thought as he laid there looking at her while she curled up next to him.

What had only seemed like minutes passed, but Erick woke to the realization that several hours had lapsed. Damani was talking on the phone, and Erick laid there quietly, half asleep, and rubbed her warm naked body as she lay next to him.

When she finished the call, she said she had to leave. Erick wondered if she would return, and quickly dismissed the idea.

Damani explained she needed to check on her family and change clothes, but she would return within the hour. She insisted he be ready when she returned so they might have lunch together.

Damani put on Erick's shirt, which was way too big for her small frame, but he smiled as he admired how well it looked on her.

Damn, that shirt has never looked better! That's sexy! He thought to himself in light of his newest conquest wearing his clothes. *The way she ties it up was kind of sexy.* She pulled some slippers out of her purse, put on her jeans, grabbed her phone and keys, and rushed out the door.

Wait, he thought to himself, *she left her stuff? I guess she really wanted me to know she was actually coming back.* About quarter to Noon Damani returned to Erick's hotel room, but without his shirt.

"Where's my shirt?" Erick inquired.

"Papi, that's my shirt now, for me to sleep in at home, and think of you."

Well, Erick thought, *I guess this is a good sign but I'm sure glad it wasn't one of my expensive shirts.*

CHAPTER 5
ZACK ARRIVES
(LA JEFA'S OFF TO WORK)

It was a beautiful day in the Dominican Republic. The sun was shining, it was hot as hell, birds were chirpings, and kids were at play. To Erick, things seemed a little brighter after a good night of great sex.

Colors were brighter, food tasted better, beer seemed colder, and birds seemed to sing a bit louder. Perhaps this was all fantasy, or residual euphoria, but it sure felt that way to Erick; and his vacation was just getting started!

It was now noon and Zack's plane wasn't scheduled to arrive until that afternoon at 4. Damani decided to take Erick to her favorite restaurant for lunch while they waited for his partner in crime to arrive. Damani was very attractive in her outfit - not dressed up like the night before - but in some short-shorts and a tank top. Erick's mind lingered on the previous evening's events, and it took all he could muster to resist the urge to take her back to his room for another round or two.

After a short walk to her favorite restaurant, they sat and enjoyed more great conversation and a delicious meal.

Damn, this is just too good to be true. Erick told himself. *I can't wait until Zack meets this chick to see what he thinks of her. For real she could be the one and I could take her home and meet my moms.*

Over lunch, Damani mentioned that she had some family business to take care of later that day, so after lunch she wanted to go gather her things from his hotel room. This would allow Erick to relax and wait for Zack to arrive. They both confessed that once Zack arrived, they were going to be full-throttle, pedal-to-the-metal, making up for the prior day he had missed. There was a lot Erick wanted to show Zack around town.

She agreed that it would be best if he showed Zack around while she ran errands, and she agreed to meet up with them later on that night.

"Do you really have to work today?" Erick pouted and made his saddest face.

"Awe, Don't worry Papi, I will find you. You are mine" she said.

After the meal and a short walk in the blazing sun, both Erick and Damani welcomed the cool air-conditioned room and the comfortable bed. They watched music videos on television. After 10 minutes of lying there together on the bed, their concentration was more on each other as they began to rip each other's clothes off. The music on the television provided the soundtrack to another great session of sex until they both passed out.

"Boom Boom Boom", a loud knock on the door woke both Damani and Erick up. Damani threw on one of Erick's shirts and answered the door. Zack stood there with a puzzled look on his face. His confused expression revealed that Damani answering the door, instead of his right-hand man, had left him questioning whether he had the right room. He looked down at a slip of paper and checked the number, but before he could look up from it, Damani laughed and helped solve the mystery.

"Are you looking for my boyfriend Erick?"

"Papi," she yelled into the room, "your friend Zackary is here." She pulled Zack close and gave him a big hug.

Okay! Finally my boy has arrived. Watch out world! Easy Trouble is back together again! Erick was excited to see his friend. Although they talk often, a few months had passed since they actually had seen each other.

Zack didn't miss a beat. He acknowledged Damani, nodded at Erick who was still lying in the bed, and went off to put his bags in his room, giving Erick and Damani time to get dressed again.

Upon his return to the room, Zack was asked by Damani to keep females away from Erick. He was *hers*, and Zack agreed. Unseen by Damani, he raised an eyebrow in Erick's direction. Erick could see Zack was ready for an explanation of the events that led to him arriving to such a strange situation.

Erick, a stone-cold player had a girlfriend after only one day in the DR? Zack could smell that there was an interesting story behind this chain of events.

Erick was excited to see his boy, and of course he wanted to tell him all about the first day there, so they decided to go to the corner bar where they could get an ice cold one, and Zack could get something to eat after his long journey from the States. Even though they said their goodbyes at the hotel, Damani walked with them to the bar. Erick kissed Damani goodbye and agreed to meet later. As she hugged Zack goodbye, Damani said she was going to bring a friend or two for Zack to meet. Jokingly, Erick blurted out, "What about me? I'm on vacation too."

With Dominican sass and finger waving, Damani replied, "No, no Papi you are mine." Erick was taken aback by how quickly she copped an attitude with him. His cousin had always warned him about those spicy Latina women with their quick attitude changes.

"Fine, you want other woman, you go," said Damani with an anguished look on her face. Erick started to laugh seeing how upset she got. He then scooped her up in his arms and told her in her ear, "Quit playing, you know you're my new Dominican girlfriend."

Zack, who was still getting adjusted to the situation he walked into, looked at Erick with a look of bewilderment. Damani kissed Erick again and told Zack "Remember he's mine. No females for him and if he does I'll cut off his balls."

"Awe, I think I'm in love. That attitude turns me on." Erick said. Zack could not hold his laughter in any longer and busted out in laughter. Erick followed, and joined him in a good laugh. They sat down at the bar and watched Damani walk up the street and out of sight.

Now, let the real fun began. Zack and Erick, Erick and Zack; Easy Trouble in the DR. Turn up!

———

Meanwhile, Damani was off to take care of family business. As she walked down the street, she checked her messages on her phone. She received twenty messages from her father and uncles. They were not used to her being unreachable, especially when it came to family business. Damani had turned her ringer off on her phone, and tucked it either under her pillow or inside her purse while she was with Erick. She definitely didn't want him to see that side of her or become suspicious of the phone ringing so much. Damani sighed and returned the most important call first.

The family was relieved that she was okay and had not been killed or kidnapped by a rival family. Her father warned her that although they knew everyone in town, had cops on payroll, and military on speed-dial, Damani still had to be careful. Her father explained to her that this is business... family business....and there was no time to be messing around. Too much money was at stake. Not to mention, there was the family reputation to uphold. Damani acknowledged her father's position, gathered her uncles, and started off to make the daily rounds to collect.

During the ride to a nearby town, Damani thought of only Erick. She couldn't stop daydreaming about spending time with him and Zack later that evening. She was smiling thinking about the night and morning they spent together. She could feel his hands all over her body. Suddenly, the truck jerked to a stop and harshly snapped Damani back to reality.

"Que Pasa?" she screamed to the driver. He explained that the road ahead was blocked by a farmer and his cattle. Damani hopped out of the truck, pulled her gun from her holster and fired two shots in the air. Startled by the noise, the farmer and his cattle meandered off the road.

Damani pointed at the driver, "Next time two shots will be in your ass and I'll find myself another driver."

She slammed the door and settled back into the backseat. Before long, Damani drifted back off to "La La land" again. She realized distractedly that the truck is no longer moving and she must have arrived at the first pick-up.

———

Damani hopped out of the truck and walked into the first bodega. As she approached, the store owner quickly appeared from behind the counter handing her the payment.

"Why is my envelope so light?" she said, clearly unhappy.

Now kneeling, head hung low, his eyes fixed on the ground, his voice quivering, he replied, "La Jefa, I am sorry. There is a guy that has been causing trouble in the neighborhood. He is saying that the towns' people must buy from him and not you."

"Pick him up," she ordered. In a stern voice "If you are lying to me I will string you up and use you for target practice. Who is this guy you speak of?"

The owner quickly sputtered out "Rocko, his name is Rocko".

Instead of taking the money from the owner, she returned the envelope, and instructed him to buy something nice for his wife and kids. So unlike her, her uncles' could only look at her with confused faces. The owner thanked her and quickly ran off. Damani got in the truck, and they drove off to the second store. They received the same story about a guy named "Rocko" here too.

"Now I see we have a problem," she murmured under her breath. Damani thought to herself, *I need to find this guy Rocko.*

"Take me to the children," she ordered the driver. Damani pulled up to the futbol pitch where some kids played. The children came running to the truck, and she handed them each 1000 pesos.

"Somebody tell me where I can find Rocko."

The children of the slums are the eyes and ears. Damani knew if she paid them, they would tell her anything. The only loyalty they have is to the Peso, but they all knew who *La Jefa* was. If *La Jefa* is asking, then they are going to tell. One of the children began to speak up.

"Come here" she said. "Take me to your house."

She asked for a shirt and pants from the mother of the child, and she put them on. The uncles looked at her. *What did she have up her sleeve now they wondered?*

She assured the mother that her son would not be in any danger. They hopped in the truck, Damani had the little boy point out where Rocko hangs out. They parked the truck about two blocks away. She sent the boy ahead to see if Rocko is indeed there. The little boy approaches Rocko, bought a few cigars, and then returned to the truck and Damani.

He reported all the necessary information that any spy would in these situations; how many guys are in the store, what each was wearing, and where they were positioned.

"It doesn't matter. All that are with him are dead," she decreed. She hopped out the truck dressed in the clothes of the little boy's mother. She wrapped her head to, looking as if she was one of the ladies who resided in the slums. She walked down the block, and tucked her gun under her shirt. She approached the store Rocko has taken over, took a deep breath and walked inside.

Rocko was a tall, built, Haitian guy. He yelled to Damani, "You woman."

Damani pointed to her chest inquisitively.

"Yes, you. I haven't seen you here before. Who are you?"

With her head turned to the floor, she explained she was visiting her sick uncle and needed to buy medicine. Rocko walked closer and smacked her butt. Damani cringed and gritted her teeth.

Damani spoke up, "no trouble, I don't want any trouble I only want to buy medicine for my sick dad." Meanwhile, she scoped the place out and ensured the little boy's report was accurate. A second man approached, Damani recognized him.

"I thought you said you need the medicine for your sick Uncle. You just said for your sick dad." He says with a confused look.

Damani tried to clean up her mistake.

"Yes, it's my Uncle. He is like my dad." The guy looked Damani up and down. He was from another town the Cruz family had dealings with in the past. She turned her head down more, and her chin almost touched her chest. Rocko rubbed on Damani's butt again. Again, she gritted her teeth, "Please hurry, he is very sick and needs this medicine."

"Man, get that medicine for this worthless bummy Bitch. She doesn't even have enough meat on her ass for a good fuck. I bet you her pussy even births flies," Rocko joked aloud.

As he handed her the medicine, he saw the diamond necklace just under her shirt. The women of the slums do not have jewelry, and certainly not necklaces like this one. His eyes widened, and before he could blurt out her identity and a warning, Damani dropped the medicine, pulled her knife from her sleeve, and sliced the man's throat.

He fell to his knees, his blood sprayed from his neck as he clutched furiously to contain it and apply pressure to the canyon she had carved. He weakened instantly, dropped, and died choking himself in an effort to stop the bleeding.

Rocko was frozen solid, immobilized with fear, as he watched his man fall to the ground. Without hesitation, Damani pulled her. 380 caliber gun out, and put two shots in Rocko's chest. The impact of the bullets hitting his chest sent him crashing through the glass countertop. Damani stood over Rocko and admired her handy work as he laid on his back looking toward the heavens, with blood oozing from his chest, and blood sputtering between his lips.

"This is Cruz family territory. Let this be a warning and lesson to all!" She put one more shot in the middle of his forehead. Damani then emptied his pockets, cleaned off her knife on his shirt, tucked her gun back under her shirt, spat on his dead bloody body, and exited the store as if nothing had happened.

The townspeople gathered outside after hearing the gun shots, as did Damani's uncles. They were there just in case she wasn't the one walking out the door after the smoke cleared.

Whispers sounded throughout the crowd, "La Jefa is inside with Rocko."

Suddenly, out walked *La Jefa* covered in blood from head to toe. There were concerned looks on the faces of the crowd.

"Don't worry," she smirked, "It's not my blood. And, by the way, you have 10 minutes to empty out the store before it goes up in flames. This is my gift to you since I am in such a motherfucking good mood."

The crowd looked at one another and quickly looted the store. One man had even taken the shoes off the feet of the dead men.

"No need for these to go to waste," he said as he morbidly giggled.

Damani signaled to her Uncles, "Burn that bitch down and let's go."

The police arrived to a crowd of people surrounding a burnt up building.

"Any casualties?" a policeman inquired.

One man spoke up from the back of the crowd, "Two sir, but they did not make it out of the fire in time."

The crowd quickly disbursed, and no one said another word about the matter. They knew the wrath of crossing *La Jefa*.

CHAPTER 6
FUN IN THE SUN (WHAT A NIGHT)

"Vamanos! Go, go, go!" yelled the tour guide.

Erick looked at Zack, Zack at Erick, and in a split second Erick revved his ATV and took off down the Dominican dirt road. Not far behind, Zack followed as they trailed the tour guide down the winding dirt road, through the sugar cane fields, over the Dominican hills, and then suddenly before them appeared the ocean.

"Park the ATVs on the sand and it's time for lunch…and a beer," yelled the Tour guide.

"Wow Z, this is the life," Erick said as he dismounted his soiled and muddy ATV.

They too, sat covered in dirt and mud at the tiny restaurant on the beach.

Erick continued on, "2 pm while all the other schmucks are at work, here we are, sitting on the beach by the ocean in the Dominican Republic, having a cold beer with our lunch. All while covered in mud. Life is good!"

He turned towards the waitress, and gave his order, "Mida, Tres Tequila por favor. Give one to the guide and the other goes to my amigo Zack, gracias."

Erick stood on a chair covered in mud, his drink held up in the air, ready to make a toast.

"It's always good to get away from the 9 to 5 and the grind of everyday life. Blessed! We work hard, we play hard. That's our motto. Grind to shine. If we don't do it for us who is going to do it? Exactly no one! Salute!"

The guys finished up their lunch, jumped by on their ATVs and finished their tour through the fields, and headed back to the hotel.

After each took a refreshing shower, they sat back, relaxed by the pool, and continued vacationing...and of course, drinking. The hotel happy hour had two-for-one drink specials, which made for a very happy hour indeed.

Across the pool, a lone man sat surrounded by a group of young ladies. He signaled to Erick and Zack to come over to join his party.

Of course it would be downright rude not to at least go say hello, Erick thought while simultaneously wondering where Damani was, and what she had been doing. He snapped out of it and remembered, it was *his* vacation, and she was taking care of *her* business. *Ain't nothing wrong with saying hello and having a few drinks. We'll catch up at the club later on, so no biggie.*

The music at the hotel pool bar was loud and bumping, the drinks flowed, and more and more people began to join the poolside festivities. It was yet mid-evening, and there was a party in full effect. They toasted to life and to happiness.

"This is the life! Funny you meet people from all over the world," Erick told Zack.

There were a couple of gentlemen from England, one from California, and even a few from New York. One of the partiers remarkably lived only 20 minutes away from Erick in Washington DC.

All of these folks meeting in the Dominican Republic, having a good time, without a care in the world, Erick continued to think.

Before long, the sun had set, and the pool party began to wind down. Erick and Zack decided to get cleaned up and dressed for the evening, called Damani and her friend, and set up a time to meet them for dinner and more fun.

Almost dressed, Zack knocked on the door. "You ready? Is Damani here yet?" he asked through the door.

"Almost ready, just need to throw on my sneakers and I'll put on my shirt when we are about to leave. I don't want to sweat it out yet" Erick said as he stood shirtless. He glanced at Zack's shirt and acknowledged to himself that he had made the right decision. Zack had already perspired a great amount from such a short walk, just three doors down the hallway, and his shirt had confirmed the humidity was all too high.

"Got to love the Dominican Republic, even after the sun goes down the weather is still nice. 80 degrees, a slight breeze coming off the ocean, and a soaked shirt. How can you beat that?" Zack said with an admission as he looked down at his shirt.

There were three loud knocks on the room door. *Boom! Boom! Boom!*

Laughter followed, as Zack opened the door with caution and revealed the source of the giggling – Damani – and behind her, a friend who was to be Zack's date for the evening.

Damani looked beautiful. Her hair was flowing gently down to her shoulders, and her body was wrapped in a fine, short, purple dress which revealed plenty of her sunned Dominican legs.

Damani turned around, giggling, and said, "Do you like what you see Papi?"

Erick stood mesmerized. *Damn, if she doesn't look like a model!* He nodded yes, and resisted the urge to pick her little ass up and throw her savagely to the bed. It took every ounce of strength he had to resist, but he knew it was going to be a good night already.

Erick failed to realize that his mouth had dropped wide open because Damani playfully slapped him back to reality and said sternly "No Papi she is for Zackary. You are mine."

Candy stood there in all of her glory; cocoa-brown skin, 5'2 and weighed no more than 120 pounds. She too, was dressed to a "T," wearing a black, skin-tight dress that seemed to be sewn on it was so tight.

Damn, this chick is fine, thought Zack, *and my type of woman!*

Damani introduced the guys to Candy. "This is Erick, the one I was telling you about, and this is his amigo Zackary."

Zack put his hand out to shake hers, but she gave him a big hug, and followed it with a kiss on the cheek. Zack's face lit up with surprise. Erick busted out in laughter when he saw Zack taken off guard totally by Candy's affection. Damani whistled, and Zack looked in Erick and Damani's direction with a grin which stretched from ear to ear.

"Are you blushing," Erick joked.

"Papi, my love, are we ready to go?" Damani said seductively.

Erick nodded, she grabbed his shirt off the chair, and the group of new friends were off. Earlier in the day, Damani had phoned and told Erick and Zack to forgo making reservations because she wanted to take them to her favorite restaurant. The four of them hopped in the cab in front of the hotel which promptly sped about the street and landscapes and quickly arrived at El Toro Restaurante.

El Toro? The bull? I wonder what type of food they have. Erick thought.

"Hola Damani and Welcome friends!" The waiter greeted them as he held the door wide open. "Right this way. We have your favorite table waiting for you."

Erick quickly glanced over the menu to find his favorite go-to South American meal; Arroz con Pollo, while Zack ordered ribs.

While waiting for their food, Erick felt a little hand on his thigh which playfully he moved off. *Oh so you want to play games?* He took his hand and slid his fingers softly along Damani's inner thigh. Damani had the same idea, because somehow without anyone knowing, she had slipped off her underwear and placed them in Erick's pocket. She took his hand and placed it on her freshly waxed bikini line, and then moved it directly atop her vagina.

"Yeah, what was that Zack? Weather is great." Erick found himself fumbling for words in light of his current situation.

Zack shot a weird look in Erick's direction.

"Dude huh?" Erick tried to maintain a straight face, but was having difficulty stifling laughter. He noticed, as Zack answered him, he too had a *guilty* look on his face. Erick wondered if they were playing the same game under-the-table game. Erick never asked and Zack never told.

"Papi, come with me. I want to show you my favorite painting in the restaurant." Erick and Damani excused themselves from the table and began to walk towards the back of the restaurant. Suddenly, Damani snatched Erick by the wrist and led him into the women's bathroom.

"There Papi, look, my favorite painting."

On the wall, Erick saw a quant painting of a semi-nude woman holding a water vase atop her head. Erick, however, had no interest in the bathroom painting. The only work of art he wanted to analyze in more detail was Damani's Dominican body.

With her panties still in his pocket, he snatched her by the back of the neck, turned her entire body around, and forced her body to pivot at the waist. Damani soon found herself face-to-face with the painting as Erick drove her short purple dress up to the middle of her back. As Damani laid bent over the sink, the door opened and an old lady walked in while he was deep inside her.

Damani and Erick both looked up in total shock. The old woman glanced down at Damani, then at Erick, smiled, and then scuttled off into a stall behind them. Erick withdrew, pulled her dress back into place, and the couple fixed their disheveled clothing to their own liking. They exchanged a smile themselves, opened the door, Erick sighed loudly, and they headed back to the table.

Oh good, the food just arrived, Erick thought. *I've worked up a little bit of an appetite.*

While the men ate their favorite dishes, Damani and Candy indulged in their own; a Dominican soup; a blend of seafood and rice.

That is probably how they stay so small and fit, Erick thought. *They do seem to be enjoying it. I might have to try that next time.*

Zack looked at Erick, and then at Damani. "Both of y'all look guilty as hell. What did y'all do? Can't let you two go off by yourselves for a minute."

Erick and Damani both refused to answer the question. Instead, they turned towards their plates and began eating their meal.

Candy blurted out, "I know what they did … I know Damani's look!" Candy then put her hands together, and signaled the two had been engaged in a sexual act.

Erick, unfazed and with a straight face, ignored Candy and her sexual innuendos, and asked, "Zackary how's your food?"

Damani blushed, Candy laughed loudly, and then pretended as if she was having an orgasm.

"Alright, Alright", Erick said, and tried his best to divert the conversation elsewhere…anywhere. "Let's toast to a good night and new amigos."

It was late, but Damani said she had a surprise for Erick and Zack before they went out dancing; one of her favorite bars. That surprise turned out to be a cab ride to the next town. The music bumped through the walls as they stood in front of a building with a large neon sign which read, *La Fantasies*.

Upon entry, the four of them were escorted to a table. The waitress took their drink orders, and Erick and Zack looked around. The men exchanged glances and smirks with each other, both came to the realization that this new *bar* was a strip club.

"Awe Zack, she loves me!"

Zack busted out into laughter. "It took you long enough," he said in reply, "but maybe you have finally met your equal half way around the world."

Damani whispers in Erick's ear, "I know you are on vacation. Maybe we can pick a girl for us later."

Huh? For us? I have to tell Zack what she said. Was this a test? Ok she is beyond too cool. What the fuck? Ok, I think I am really falling for this chick.

As Erick and Damani watched the women dance on stage, they began to once again explore each other's bodies and the lack of limitations, under the table. Erick pushed further and further, and soon felt the moistness on his fingers as he slowly stroked Damani's lips.

Damani began panting and breathing heavily, and then leaned in for a kiss and found her way to Erick's jeans.

Erick was taken aback by the openness, both sexually and publicly, that Damani displayed. He thought to himself, *it was good thing I have on a long shirt.*

Erick had almost forgotten that Zack was at the table until he felt a bump on his leg, possibly from a high heel. He looked over the table to see Candy had fully straddled Zack. She sucked on his neck while he cupped her ass. In addition to Candy's full-fledged assault, Zack was also getting a table dance from the stripper.

Erick mused to himself, *I guess Candy didn't want to be upstaged. That's my boy. If my hands weren't busy I would give him a high five.*

"Last call for alcohol", came over the speakers. They ordered one more round of drinks.

The strip club was shutting down? Cool. Erick didn't want to spend much more time in the club. *I can't wait to get Damani back to the hotel and break her back!*

Now just after Midnight, the group piled into a cab, and was off.

Feeling lovely and quite horny, Erick wondered, *what's Damani got planned for us next? She seems full of surprises tonight.*

After a twenty minute cab ride, they arrived at a place whose sign outside just read "Club." The outside of the "Club" was packed with people waiting to get inside, and the line wrapped around the corner. This was the popular place to be in town, and it looked as if they would not let anyone else in for a while.

As they got out of the cab however, the security guard pointed in their direction and signaled for them to come forward and approach him.

"Please wait right here," he said, as he mumbled into a walkie talkie strapped to his shoulder. In what seemed to be an instant, a waitress and security guard appeared at the door and escorted the four of them inside the "Club." Erick looked at Zack, Zack looked at Erick, and they both looked at Damani. In both shock and awe at the quick response to their arrival, they walked into the crowded club.

Diddy-boppin to the music through the club, the four made their way to a table which was just to the side of dance floor. The club was crazy packed, and filled from wall to wall with people. Reggaeton and hip-hop music played over the speakers, scantily dressed women and drinks flowed freely about.

This place was great. Erick ordered drinks from the waitress, and while they waited, he and Zack watched as Damani and Candy teased them from the dance floor with their 2 girl show. The waitress came back, but she didn't have any drinks with her… she went to Damani onto the dance floor and whispered something in her ear. Damani signaled for Erick and Zack to get up and follow the waitress as she led them to different seats.

It seemed that one of Damani's friends had offered them seats at their table. Erick and Zack obliged, but Erick insisted that they keep their own tab. Damani's new friends were very generous, and insisted on buying all of the shots of alcohol the boys could want.

"Friends of Damani's are friends of mine," Pablo said as he introduced himself, his hand outstretched for a friendly handshake. The men shook hands.

"I'm Erick and this is Zack."

Damani and Candy were ready to party, dance, and include Erick and Zack in on the fun.

"Come on Papi, "Damani said as she grabbed Erick's hand. Candy followed suit, and grabbed Zack in a similar fashion. "Let's go down to the dance floor".

Zack and Erick escorted them back down to the dance floor, and one of the other women who was seated at the table also joined the couples. As Zack got dragged onto the crowded floor with Damani, Candy and the lady from the table danced provocatively. Erick did not feel like joining the extraordinarily crowded dance floor, so he found a spot off to the side where he enjoyed his drink without getting bumped. He sat back, laughed, and cheered Zack on as he was surrounded by three dancing women.

That look on Zack's face is priceless! Erick watched. *My boy has got to have think he died and went to heaven!*

Zack rocked side to side to the beat, and danced with the three gorgeous women when suddenly a Haitian guy bumped into him. Zack was drunk, but knew enough to turn and apologize. He then returned to his dance party of four. Erick watched cautiously and at the ready. Clearly, this was not an accident, but the guy had intentionally bumped Zack.

Erick thought, *Hmmm, my spidey-sense is tingling!*

The large Haitian man then tried to dance with the girl from the table. He grabbed her forcefully around the waist, and then Damani yanked her friend free from him and said something inaudible to Erick. She waved her finger, and he knew it was something serious. From a distance, he could tell the girl too was uncomfortable with the situation, because she moved to the other side where Zack stood.

The Haitian yelled back, raised his beer toward Damani, and spilled the contents on Zack in the process. Erick shot Zack a look, nodded, and that nod meant he saw what had happened, but also told Zack to let it go.

Zack, always the lover and not the fighter, asked the guy nicely to back off. "We are just here to have a good time. If she doesn't want to dance with you she doesn't have to."

"Fuck that bitch you are with!" The Haitian yelled as he moved closer, so close, that he was inches from Zack's face.

Zack chuckled, "Okay, fuck her, but you aren't going to touch her."

Without being noticed, Erick had moved within two feet of the scuffle. *He gets one more, that's it. One more time to make threatening advances towards Zack or the girls*, Erick thought to himself.

The Haitian raised his beer angrily toward Zack, yelled something in French, and doused Zack with his beer. Zack laughed, wiped the excess liquid from his shirt, huddle the girls up to walk them off the dance floor, and back up to the table.

The guy advanced on Zack. "You American bitch!"

Those were the last words spoken by the Haitian that night in an upright position. Before he could utter another, he found himself on the ground in a daze, and a size 13 Nike shoe greeted his attempt to gain his bearings. Erick turned, and walked slowly away and joined his party back at the table; Zack had already escorted all three women safely back to their seats.

"One-hitter-quitter! Followed by the ole size 13s!" Erick said as he tried to bring his temperament back into check.

Nobody said anything to Erick or the group. By the time security got to the dance floor, Zack was back at the table with the girls and Erick had made his way back from the other side of the club. They all watched from the table as security picked up a drunk, dazed, confused Haitian and threw him out a side door.

Erick looked at Zack, and Zack at Erick. "Another story for the books huh," Erick said as he and Zack shared a laugh. Damani and the other girls excused themselves from the table. Erick, Zack and Damani's friend Pablo, each took shots of Patron.

"Fuck it homey, not going to let some guy fuck with you, spill drinks, cuss at you, and then on top of all that put hands on a woman. He deserved what he got. You know I got your back forever. Oh well, this don't stop the party."

"Salute!" Erick, Zack and Pablo raised their shot glasses, knocked them together, and threw back another shot.

"Damn my hand hurts though. Give me that bucket of ice." They all shared a laugh.

What Erick and Zack didn't know was that Damani had made a phone call when she went to the bathroom. "I want that motherfucker dead. How dare he confront me in the club while I'm out with friends" she yelled into the phone.

Candy tried to calm the hot-headed Damani, "Remember Erick and Zack are back at the table. Your new man did good… wow. I know you gonna do something special for him tonight." As she made her plea, she did a little sexy dance that made Damani burst out laughing.

"Fuck him; Jorge and Papo will deal with him later. He better be glad we are having such a good night or I would slice his throat myself," Damani said angrily.

Upon returning to the table, Damani jumped into Erick's arms. "You miss me Papi?" The other girls followed suit with their guys. "Papi let's take the bottle to finish it on the beach." The bottle was almost empty, so

Pablo suggested they get another two. They paid the tab, and headed out of the club and took the short walk down to the beach. The moon shone brightly, and glimmered off the dark waves on the ocean. The six of them sat, talked, laughed and passed round the bottle until all of the Tequila was gone. They all sat on the beach, each man embraced his woman, and they watched the sun rise before they headed back to the hotel.

"Pablo, we can get a cab" Erick stated.

Pablo insisted. "It's on our way. Besides, we have more than enough room in the truck. Why wait for a cab and spend the money? Let us take you to your hotel."

Too drunk to argue any further, the group piled into the back of the truck. The cool night air streaked through the bed of the truck, and Erick and Zack took this as an opportunity to embrace the girls. The truck rumbled through the streets, and then came to a stop in front of the hotel. Zack and the girls jumped out of the truck, said their good-byes, and briefly watched Pablo and his lady disappear into the night, down the road, and then out of sight.

"What a night Zack! We had a great day if you think about it. ATV riding during the day, good food, good drinks, strip club, and look at these women we are with. I love the Dominican Republic! All in all it was one of those days you dream of!"

Candy hugged Damani, and Erick and Zack dap hands before they headed to their separate rooms, hand in hand, with their new Dominican women.

I always keep my promises, Erick thought. *It's time to break you off a little something proper!*

He threw Damani to the bed, and quickly removed her clothes.

CHAPTER 7
A BIRTHDAY CELEBRATION

The smell of fried Plantains, eggs, sausages, and pancakes filled the air of the tiny 3 bedroom house. "Saulo, Saulo" his mother called to him. "Time to wake up!" she sang, and her words rang throughout the house. "Feliz Cumpleanos! Happy Birthday!"

"Today my son, how old are you?"

Enthusiastically, a little voice issued forth. He tried to deepen his voice, and bellowed out from under the covers, "13!"

Saulo lived with his mom Guadalupe, his father Juan Manual, and baby sister Gabriella. Juan Manuel ran the local convenience store while Guadalupe led a modest life as a housewife. Like many Dominican families, the man was responsible for "bringing home the bacon," while the mother tended to the household.

"Hurry up and get washed up so you can meet us at the table for breakfast."

Saulo ran quickly and washed up, then made his way to the kitchen. A smile glimmered across his face. A birthday meant that his mother would make a special pancake; one just for the birthday boy. This special pancake was something that he looked forward to every year.

Saulo's mouth watered as his mother placed his food on the table in front of them. In Saulo's plate was the one big pancake she had made especially for him.

As they settled in their seats, and prepared to eat, a loud series of knocks sounded from the front door.

Boom! Boom! Boom!

Now who could that be this early? Guadalupe thought.

Again, three louder knocks reverberated from the door to their tiny abode.

BOOM! BOOM! BOOM!

"Guadalupe, sit down. You have done enough this morning, I'll get the door," Juan Manuel said to his wife. He took the napkin he had draped across his lap, folded it neatly, and dropped it beside his plate on the table.

"Hola Como Esta?" he said as he opened the door.

Saulo got up and peeked around the corner quietly. He saw two large men stood in the doorway. He could hear them saying something to his father, but Juan Manual signaled that they should speak softer. This was unfortunate for Saulo, as he could not quite make out the conversation.

"Juan Manuel," one of the men said, "you need to come with us."

"Please," Juan Manuel begged. "Today is my son's birthday. Is it possible that we handle this another day or even another time? We are just sitting down to have breakfast."

"Look we can do this the hard way or the easy way," the large man said as he flashed a .9mm Nickel-plated pistol which rested in his waist band. "You know El Commodore doesn't like to wait."

Saulo ran and sat back at the table. He picked up his fork and began eating his special meal, and acted as if he was fully unaware of what he had just heard. His charade was interrupted suddenly as Juan Manual returned and knelt at his side.

"Son, I have to go to the store and I will be back later to celebrate with you. We will go and have shaved ice and you can pick out a new futbul."

Saulo agreed, and said, "See you later Papi"

Juan Manuel kissed Gabriella, and gave Guadalupe a big hug and several small kisses on her tiny face. "Everything is fine," he said assuredly, "I just need to sort out something at the store real quick, and I will be back later on to continue with the celebration."

A deep voice came from the front door, "Alright, alright, that's enough, Juan time to go. NOW!"

Juan Manuel gave one last hug and kiss to his wife, kissed the baby girl on the forehead, and slapped Saulo a high-five as he walked towards the door.

"I'll see you guys later."

"Papi! Papi! Don't forget you promised," yelled Saulo. He watched as his father got into a big shiny gray truck and drove away.

The next morning Saulo woke up and ran to the kitchen, "Papi?" Guadalupe sat at the table, her eyes red, tissue clutched in both hands.

"Mommy, where is Papi?"

"Papi came in late last night, and left early to go to work," she said as if speaking the lie aloud would somehow make it true.

Guadalupe gathered herself together, choked down what remaining emotion she had, and told Saulo to get dressed. They left the house and walked to the store, but it was locked and had no signs of it being opened recently. Guadalupe sighed a very heavy sigh, and said, "Come on, we have one more stop."

They walked up to a big grey building, pulled open the heavy metal door, and walked in. There they filed a "Missing Person" report with the Police, but placed a lie in the one box empty that would help them the most; "Last Known Whereabouts." She dared not say who her husband left with, but simply wrote in the space that he didn't return home from the store the previous evening.

"Hola Policia, Can I talk to you? Hello, officer?" One officer after another walked by her.

"Hello, can I... hello, my husband." Finally, one of the officers stopped, and turned in her direction.

"Can I help you ma'am?"

"My husband didn't come home last night," Guadalupe said sadly.

The police officer looked at her directly, smiled, and said hatefully, "Ma'am look a lot of husbands don't go home to their wives every night especially, if they have to come home to a nagger checking on them like you."

Disgusted by what the office said, she slapped him, and furiously reached down and took her shoes, and threw them at his head. He dodged the sandals, and laughed.

"Saulo, grab your sister. We are going."

The police officer picked up her shoes. "Ma'am don't forget your shoes!" He chuckled, and two other officers who had previously ignored her, joined him in a chorus of laughter. He tossed them in a trash can nearby, turned, and walked away.

Juan would never cheat on me, but was it possible? He has always come home every night for the last 15 years and he promised his son. He is not the type of man that would go back on a promise to his child.

She began to cry. Frustrated, she grabbed Gabby from Saulo's arms and started the long walk home, along the red dirt road, and with bare feet.

At 4 a.m., Saulo was awoken by the screams of his mother. "No! No! No! Juan Manuel" she yelled.

Before Saulo could fully get his bearings, a neighbor rushed into the bedroom, picked Gabby and him up, and whisked them out their bedroom.

"Where are we going," Saulo asked as he was rushed passed his mother.

As he glanced down in the flurry, he could see his mother. She knelt on the ground, a bloody blanket lay in front of her, and she screamed out in agony. "No Juan Manuel what am I going to do now? What did you get yourself into? Why? Why? Why?" she said as she sobbed uncontrollably.

The neighbor shielded Saulo's face, and forced him to look towards his shoulder. "We are going to watch you for a little bit. Your mother doesn't feel well. It's still early." He lied as lovingly as possible. The neighbor laid the two children down on his couch, draped them in blankets, and sang softly.

Guadalupe cried loudly. She shook, but pulled the sheet back to reveal what she already knew to be. Under the sheet laid Juan Manuel, lifeless and bloody. He had been badly beaten, his body bruised in more places than not, and a gaping wound stretched under his chin; ear to ear, they had sliced Juan Manual's neck.

CHAPTER 8
THE RETURN OF SAULO

Saulo Rodriquez, now Special Agent Rodriquez, had a chip on his shoulder since that day, his terrible 13th birthday, the day he became the man of the household. As he grew, Saulo watched his mother struggle as she raised two children without a father.

Guadalupe tried to get a job at a resort, but didn't have the proper documentation needed, nor did she have the money to get them. She tried to bartend, but found that she couldn't make even the simplest of drinks. Her attempt to waitress failed as well; she dropped too many orders. She once tried to be a mule for a drug smuggler, but lost her courage before she could pass through security, and walked right back out the airport terminal. She tried to be a runner, but kept getting robbed.

Life was tough, and her failures came easy. She had all but given up on life, and even frequented the bars in search of a gringo to be a sugar-daddy to her and her kids. She couldn't stand the old white men with old balls. She refused to sell herself anymore.

One day a neighbor mentioned that La Cruz Familia was looking for maids and house help. Neighbors often whispered about this decision, questioning, *how could she go work for the people that were rumored to kill her husband?*

She had even questioned herself, but concluded, *you do the things that you have to do when you have children. If it was just me, I surely could have made it another way. But when your family is accustomed to a certain lifestyle, then you try your best to maintain it. It was bad enough Juan Manuel is no longer around.*

Saulo could not live with his father murder being unsolved. At a young age, Saulo would go with his mother to a big house on the hill where the Cruz family lived. He was extremely jealous of the daughter, Damani.

She had everything one could ever want. All she had to do was ask. He remembered on Damani's 16th birthday she asked for a horse, and she got a horse. Saulo had received no horse that year or any other, but his 16th birthday brought him a used soccer ball, new underwear, and some socks.

He both hated and envied her and the Cruz family. Damani always cared for Saulo though. She snuck him extra food and candy when nobody was looking. Whatever she had he had. Sometimes, it seemed, Damani wanted nothing more but to be a *regular* kid. Saulo developed a huge crush on Damani, and although she really liked him as well, she also knew her father would disapprove of her dating *the help's son.* They had kept their love for one another a secret from their families and each other.

Guadalupe made sure that her children wanted for nothing. She worked long hours at the house as the maid. She eventually became so indispensable that the family asked her to become a live-in maid.

Saulo hated how they treated her. He felt his mother was just more than a servant to the rich and powerful. He vowed to her on one occasion, "One day I will get them back for treating you that way."

As he said this, he felt a stinging sensation on the side of his face. She had smacked him instantly.

"Don't you ever say that, or let me hear you say that again."

"But mom…"

"Don't, *but mom* me. Nothing!" She continued…" I am very fortunate to have a job. Who knows what I would be doing? Were you taking care of me and your sister, the bills, or putting food on the table?"

"But mom…"

She cut him off again, "What I need you to do is leave this place. I have saved enough money to send you to live with your uncle in Santiago. This way you at least can have a fresh start."

Not long after Damani's 16th birthday, Saulo was to be sent away to Santiago to live with his Uncle. Before leaving, they met under the stars, as they often did, for one last time. Then, as quickly as Saulo came into Damani's life, he was gone.

Although they were not the best living conditions, Saulo left to his uncle's in Santiago. This new opportunity afforded him the chance to get a good education in a safe environment. At 17 years of age, he was allowed to join the Dominican Army. After breezing through basic training and becoming a decorated marksman, Saulo was recruited to join the Elite Task force. He was a perfect match for this branch of the military with his Type-A personality traits; competitive, aggressive, controlling, and overly ambitious.

After years of training with the Elite Task force, he was finally given the approval to become a full-fledged member. The boy once known as Saulo was now 25 years-old and Special Agent Saulo Rodriquez.

His commanding officer took full advantage of Saulo's leadership skills and decided he was ready to head up a team in the Task Force. The first assignment he drew was to identify the key players involved in the corruption of his old town. He was very excited because this was a chance for him to return home, get reacquainted with his mother, his sister, and Damani.

His mother still worked for La Familia Cruz after all these years. Saulo boldly walked up to the Cruz compound with eyes on looking. Not just anyone just walks up onto the compound.

"I am here to see Guadalupe," he demanded.

"And who the hell are you?" the doorman responds with uncertainly.

"Tell her, her son has returned home."

Of course, he had to tell a lie to his own mother about why he was returning home, but nevertheless he was happy to see her. She wept tears of joy when she first laid eyes on him. She ran up to him, hugged him tightly and kissed him. Her hands explored his face lovingly.

"Mom it's me."

"Saulo, Oh my how much you have grown and become a man."

Saulo was a handsome, neat, well-groomed Dominican man. He was physically fit weighting 185 pounds and standing an even 6'0. He took pride in his appearance and always tried to look his best. Saulo was given the nickname *Pretty Boy* during basic training by his commanding officers.

"You look so much like your father, God rest his soul. He would be so proud to see how much you have grown. What have you been doing with yourself?"

Saulo explained that he had gone to school, learned carpentry, and now has returned back home to help with the ongoing construction in the town. He had heard there were good opportunities here and lots of money to be made. The reunion was short lived. Suddenly a loud voice came over the intercom speaker, "Guadalupe, El Commodore needs you."

"Saulo, wait here and I will be right back with you."

About 20 minutes passed and Guadalupe returned crying to the maids' quarters where Saulo had been waiting for her.

"What is wrong mother?"

"Nothing Saulo, leave it alone."

"Mother what happened?" he demanded an answer.

"Saulo, leave it alone… its nothing. Please you do not know these people. I've heard things, seen things. Terrible things and I don't want you involved and I don't want to lose my job. So please I pray, as she pulls a rosary from under her shirt. I pray that you do not get involved with them and you find a good job working elsewhere."

She performed a prayer while holding Saulo's hand. "The father, the son, the holy ghost, keep my son safe and out of trouble. Thank you for bringing him back to me after all these years. I am so happy to see him. Amen." She finished her prayer and then looked back to Saulo. "Your sister is going to be ecstatic when she lays eyes on you. She probably won't even know who you are."

Guadalupe kissed Saulo. "Son, meet me back here at 9pm and we can go catch up and have some food and drinks at Lolita's Bar. I must show you off to my friends. Awe my son, I love you, but I must return back to work. See you later, besos (kisses)."

Saulo left his mother with the promise to meet up with her after work. As he walked down the street, he noticed a beautiful woman getting out of a SUV truck. As he walked a little closer, he thought, *she looks like my old friend Damani. Man, has she changed. How different she looks…totally grown up now. It has been some years, I look quite different too.*

He stared at her from afar. He was now convinced that this was her. She looked good, better than he could remember. The feelings he had for her rushed back. He couldn't contain his excitement, and yelled out "DAMANI!" from across the street. As she peered across the street to see who was screaming her name, her hand moved quickly to her waistband, and to her gun. He ran across the street, but was met by Papo's gun, pointed at him, and pointed directly in his face.

"Who the fuck are you? Pretty Motherfucker, back up!" Papo demanded.

Saulo raised his hands in the air, looked in Damani's direction, and said, "It is me Saulo, Saulo Rodriguez, your old friend. My mom works as a maid at your house. Remember, we use to sneak and eat cookies and candy from the kitchen. We use to go and spy on the older kids at the swimming hole. We played when we were kids, don't you remember? I'm back in town."

As he continued to speak, Damani commanded her uncle, "Uncle Papo lower your weapon."

"So are you single? Any children?" he said jokingly.

"Look Saulo, I don't have time for this. Don't come approaching me on some Baby-how-you-been-shit, I am back in town. It has been over 15 years since I have seen you. No letters or anything from you. I did not know what was up with you or if you were even alive. Yes I am single, No I don't have any children, but like I said I am very busy right now and I must be going to check in with my father right now. See you around."

The girl he once knew seemed very, very different now, and he liked it. Saulo couldn't believe that Damani just didn't fall into his arms upon being reunited with him. *Did she see me? I know I look good?* Saulo thought with arrogance. *I'm not worried, I just need to put in a little effort and she will love me forever.*

CHAPTER 9

BRUNCH

It was Sunday morning, and Erick woke up as Damani ended her phone call. "Good Papi! You are awake. Call Zackary's room and tell him let's go have brunch at my friends place and spend the day at the beach."

"Shit. Sounds good to me. A day of relaxation, especially after having to hit that motherfucker at the bar last night. Let me call Zack right now," he said as he picked up the phone.

Zack came down the stairs to Erick's room with Damani's friend Candy from the previous night still draped over him.

"Look at Zack's face! They must have had a good night," Erick joked to Damani.

"Papi leave them alone, and let them enjoy themselves. Let's go. It's a short walk to my friend's house." They collected their belongings, and started the walk.

Where in the world is this woman taking us? Erick thought.

They had left the concrete roads and were now walking on loose gravel, dirt, and clay roads that led them through the sugar cane fields. Damani stopped, pulled at one of the canes shooting skyward, broke a piece off, bit into it, and offered Erick some; "Here Papi try it."

"Naw," Erick said with a look of disgust about his face, "Naw I'm good."

Damani threw the sugar cane stick to Candy who took a bite. Zack immediately waved off the notion of even trying it before an offer could be made. Damani and Candy continued to chew on the sugar cane, chattered in Spanish, and then pointed and laughed in Zack and Erick's direction. Erick and Zack shrugged shoulders, looked at each other, and began to laugh also.

"Damani, baby how much longer?" Erick inquired.

She made some motion which seemed to mean something and nothing at once, lifted up her dress teasingly, and he became distracted. He ran up to her, scooped her into his arms, and swirled her around in the field. Suddenly, Zack said, "Yo, E chill."

"Zack, what's wrong with you? We were just having a little fun?"

Erick, having turned towards Zack, noticed the look of concern on his face. He slowly turned to look in the direction of his gaze, and was stunned to find two guys on either side of the four of them, holding guns, big guns, at that.

That's some military grade type shit, thought Erick. *Great, an escort, in a sugar cane field, with machine guns.*

The jubilant smiles had disappeared from Zack and Erick.

Erick grabbed Damani's arm, pulled her closer, and whispered, "Yo que pasa mami?"

"Calm down Papi," she said loudly. "Pay them no mind. These are my friends. My friends are your friends. OK. OK."

"I thought we were just going to have brunch at your friend's house on the beach?" Erick asked incredulously.

"We are."

As they rounded the next corner, a beautiful mansion came into view. It had been hidden by the tall green sugar canes, and only a few steps in the right direction revealed a marvelous structure. Erick and Zack's mouths dropped wide open as they saw the mansion for the first time.

"Hey Erick and Zack, you remember my friend Pablo from the bar last night? And this is his wife Alexandria," Damani said as she made the proper introductions.

I had no idea that lady from the bar last night was Pablo's wife, Erick thought. *I thought that she was just Pablo's date. Damn, she is gorgeous! I just thought I was doing some random chick a favor; preventing harassment and all!*

The woman stood 5'10, model-like thin, not boney, but slender with long beautiful brown hair and hazel eyes. As they talked, she disclosed that she was mixed between African American and Dominican. Her skin radiated with this perfect mixture, as she explained her father's relocation from America to join her mother in the DR.

Erick stood, gazing at this woman, and tried to work this mystery out in his mind. *How in the hell did Pablo pull this woman? He couldn't be able to pull a woman like this under normal circumstances. Maybe it's something in the water? Maybe it has something to do with his bankroll? They are definitely the oddest couple I've seen.*

Standing only 5'7, Pablo was short but stocky. He looked like the type of guy that others underestimated in a fight, but wound up revealing the strength of an ox and upsetting all challengers.

Erick continued to piece the puzzle together internally. *I definitely am not going to take any chances with him. Especially since we just got escorted through fields by machine-gun toting farm hands. I wonder what kind of farm he's running anyways.*

The group was quickly escorted onto the grounds of the estate. Pablo and Alexandria showed them around a beautifully decorated house, and Damani and Candy excused themselves from the tour they had witnessed innumerable times. They headed towards the beach, and the bright shining sun.

As Pablo led Zack into a room to show him a collection of cars, Erick had lagged behind to look at a painting on the wall. *This looks like a Basquiat. I'll check it out later against the internet's resident experts*, he thought.

He pulled out his phone, turned on the camera application, and snapped a few pictures of the painting. As he did, he felt a hand on his ass. He turned around and expected it to be Damani, but the hand belonged to the hostess, Alexandria.

"Whoa", Erick stuttered in total shock. "What are you doing?" He gently, but quickly, grabbed her hand and positioned it next to her hip and away from his own.

"Oh I like American men." Her hand quickly moved back towards Erick, and his zipper. "They turn me on so much. I just wanted to say *thank you* for saving me from that guy last night."

Alexandria grabbed Erick's hand this time, and led him out onto the balcony, away from everyone else, and quickly maneuvered her hand down his pants and to his manhood. Erick seemed stunned, but then quickly caught sight of Damani as she ran to the ocean, excused himself and ran after her.

"I'll catch up with you later."

Erick ran out the house, down the hot sandy beach, and left a trail of clothes along the way. He reached Damani as a big wave crashed to shore, tackled her in the water, and relaxed.

They both thought the water felt good after the long walk in the hot sun. Their moment of reprieve didn't last, and before long, they were signaled by Pablo.

"I guess lunch must be ready," Damani said as she pulled him from the water. "Come on Papi!"

As they made their way back up to the house, a spread of food was being laid out on the table at the pool-side. The table held a view that overlooked the waves, the endless ocean before them, and a bevy of fish, fresh fruit, salad, rice, beans, and chicken crowded the table.

"Alexandria, I know you and the girls will want some wine, so go and get two bottles out of the wine cellar. Also bring a few beers for the guys," Pablo ordered.

Erick looked at Zack, and Zack returned it.

"This is the way to live. We need to definitely figure out fast how we can live here, in a house like this, with a private beach."

"Ditto! " Zack nodded his head in agreement.

All six of them laughed, joked, ate and drank for what seemed to be hours.

"I am beyond stuffed." Erick admitted to the group.

"No more. I am tapping out too." Zack grabbed his stomach, and then shook his head in agreement with Erick.

Pablo insisted, "You have to have some dessert!"

Damani got up from her chair, kissed Erick's lips, and whispered, "Papi, I will see you later." The other girls followed suit with their respective men.

"Me, the girls, and this bottle of wine are going to go for a walk on the beach. You stay, talk and enjoy. We won't be long." As the men watched, the girls prance and dance off down the beach.

Pablo spoke up. "Damani loves you," he said as he smiled in Erick's direction.

"Why do you say that?"

"She is so happy when she is around you. I have never seen her like that. She is like my sister. My family has done business with her family for as long as we can remember. Alexandria did not tell me until we got home what you did for her in the club last night."

"If you ever need a job, you can come and work with me. I will definitely make it worth your while. You guys definitely need to come back and visit. Whenever you are in town, you make sure you come and at least say hello. I like the way that you carry yourself and how smart you are. Both you and Zack would be very valuable to my company for international trade."

"But, enough about business right now." Pablo pulled out three cigars, and held them up in his left hand. In his right, he grabbed the bottle of Tequila from the table and raised it too.

"I'll respectfully decline on the cigar, but absolutely will take a drink of tequila."

"Zack, how about you?" Pablo inquired.

"Only tequila for me also," Zack replied.

Pablo chuckled, and poured three shot glasses full of the cold tequila until they overfilled. "What's mines is yours... Salute!"

"Salute!" The three cheered as their glasses clinked together in unison.

Erick wondered if Pablo really meant that. *What's mine is yours! If you only knew,* he chuckled to himself. He thought about the episode with Alexandria on the balcony just hours prior, then quickly dismissed his little inside joke before he might accidentally say something that he would regret.

Pablo, Erick and Zack laughed, talked about sports and cars until the sun disappeared behind the house. As the sun set, and the pool lights flickered on, the Dominican sky over the ocean was beautiful; filled with purples, reds, and oranges.

As they giggled like school girls, the three tipsy women casually strolled back to the table. "Did you miss us?" they all said in unison. "We know you did" as they hugged and plopped down sloppy in the respective lap of their counterpart.

After a long relaxing Sunday of great conversation, food, drinks and company, the group parted ways. Pablo was a little tipsy himself, and rambled on, "My two new American amigos, I love you guys!" He threw one arm around Erick, and the other around Zack, kissed them both on the cheek, and then burst into a song.

Zack and Erick both laugh as they unexpectedly received a kiss on the cheek from their host.
"Now promise me you will meet us at the club later. I'll get a table. Remember what we talked about."

Erick and Zack promised to meet Pablo and Alexandria at the club later that night. "As soon as we recharge, we are there!"

Pablo insisted they allow his associate to drive them home, and even offered to have to have them picked up later that night. Since the club was only a few blocks down from the hotel Erick and Zack declined, but assured the couple that the group would meet them there.

"What a day!" Zack said.

Erick nodded his head in agreement. "What about that house?" Erick said with amazement. "I think we need to step it up a level if we are ever going to get to Pablo's status!"

Zack agreed with a single nod of his head.

CHAPTER 10

TASK FORCE

In a small warehouse located in Cabarete, two towns over from the target location in Puerto Plata, there gathered 10 individuals. Each puzzled as to why they have been summoned to meet at such a location and at such an hour. The group consisted of seven men and three women. They laughed and joked with one another as they waited for the meeting to begin.

"Whoever invited us here must have forgotten what time they said meet them here," he joked to the others from the front of the small room.

"I will give them until 10am and then I'm out of here" another said.

They all nodded in agreement. In the midst of their laughter, they had not noticed that Agent Saulo Rodriquez had entered the room, and now stood in the back. He turned his head, took inventory of who was in attendance, and listened to the continual joking.

"I don't know why you are here? I remember you from training camp... you were the slowest runner of them all."

"Ha ha! Very fucking funny! I might have been the slowest runner of them all, but I got the best record of putting a cap in someone's ass! You want to find out?"

The two trash-talkers both jumped up, pushed one another backwards, and jockeyed for the Alpha-male role in the group.

"Break it up, break it up, you two both are a bunch of nobodies," said one of the ladies as she jumped between them. "I'd make you both my bitches."

"Oooooo" rang out from the rest of the bunch.

Saulo decided he had seen enough of this feisty bunch. Saulo walked to the front of the room, kicked the chair where one of the guys had his feet up, and stood and faced the group.

"Okay, Okay, Enough! Attention!"

They all jumped up, straightened their arms stiff at their sides, and then saluted.

"Sit down, sit down. First things first, if I catch you saluting me again you are off this team."

"Well what team is this?" asked one of the Alpha-Males.

"Well, I'm glad you asked. First my name is Special Agent Saulo Rodriquez. You ten, men and women, have been brought here for a reason. You have been assigned to me as a special task force to eliminate the corruption in the area. We are not dealing with the petty thefts and/or small drugs dealers. We are looking for the major players and contributors."

"Yes, we are going after the heads of the organizations. We are going to use smart, decisive intel, by blending in with the community and gathering information and building our cases from within. In doing so, we will be able to build strong cases against these organizations; cases which will be taken to my superiors and then prosecuted. The first area we are targeting is two towns over; the northern territory of Puerto Plata."

"Each of you has been handpicked by me. You are now a team. My team. You must get along with each other because *you* are all that you have! This is all we have. We have each other and no one else we can trust. You are the best of the best, and you were handpicked to help me eliminate the ring of corruption in this region by any means necessary."

"If you don't feel like you are up for the task there is the fucking door! Don't let it hit you in the ass when you leave either. I don't want that smell to linger after you go. Now if you want the chance to make history, bust some heads open and ruin the lives of some bad guys, then this is the place for you."

They each look around to see if any of the other was getting up to leave. Nobody moved a muscle.

"Alright then, now that is out of the way. First assignment, like I mentioned, is two towns over from here. It is no secret that the police force, military, judges, politicians are all corrupt. No one under any circumstances is to know that this task force exists. You need to take every precaution to remain undercover and invisible while being visible."

"There is a box being passed around. Place your police-issued weapons and shields inside. They will be locked up in this vault. Only my boss and I have access to this safe. You will be provided with unmarked guns, and chipped untraceable cell phones. Understand that we do not know who can be trusted outside of this team. You answer to me and I answer to – well - that's not important."

"All documents and information will remain in this building. This is our headquarters. You will only be asked to check in every so often to assure that your identities are not compromised. We will have arranged times to meet. All surveillance recordings will be warehoused at this location. All pictures taken from cameras will be immediately uploaded to a server and erased from your cameras in case you need to dump a camera, or somehow you are put into a compromising position. There will be NO wires worn by this team. Do we all understand the first objective of this team?"

"Yes sir they each answered."

"Okay now that we got all of that out of the way, any questions?"

No one responded. Saulo walked up to the wall where a corkboard had been mounted three feet off the ground. He slid an envelope open, withdrew a large picture, and pulled a pin from the board. He positioned the picture at the very top of the corkboard and stuck a pin in the top of the black and white reconnaissance photo.

"Our target, who we believe is the key player in the Northern Territory of Puerto Plata, is known as Esteban "El Commodore Cruz. El Commodore, the head of the Cruz family should not be taken lightly. He and the La Cruz Familia Cartel are suspected of multiple crimes; Murder, Conspiracy, and Human and Drug Trafficking, to name just a few."

"We have three months to do as much surveillance, gather as much evidence as possible, and build a solid case against Esteban Cruz and his family."

Each member of the group was handed a manila folder with their primary target. While most of the team had been assigned to an individual target, Saulo had two members following Damani.

This devotion to Damani caused the team to believe that she was of the utmost importance to the mission, but the obsession had actually been of personal interest to Saulo. He had become so intrigued by her beauty, an opportunity missed perhaps, and yearned to find out what had happened to the girl he once knew. He thought that she was everything he could have asked for in a wife, but then the surveillance revealed that she had eyes for another.

Saulo tried to remain professional and on-task, but his questions and tactics revealed an agenda that was focused on more than just corruption and organized crime.

"Have we identified this guy in the pictures with Damani? The one she seems to be around all the time. Look here they are together in pictures one, two and three. Three times he shows up. She supposed to be single, so who is this guy? Is he a major player? Where is he from? He looks black? American? Find out who he is now!"

His obsession failed to subside. Saulo began to follow Erick and Zack undercover, on his own time, and without backup. He shifted the team from Damani, and assigned them to patrol Erick and Zack.

She had to be with this guy for a reason, he thought. *She's not allowed to date just anyone. This guy has to be somebody to get blessings from her family. What's the connection?*

Saulo dressed as a bum and beggar on the streets. He boldly walked up to them and asked for money. He watched them as they sat, relaxed, and ate lunch on the beach. He also had his team pose as different street merchants to keep an eye on Erick and Zack. All the while, his team failed to find anything of significance. He was exhausting his resources, wasting time, and it had gotten him nowhere.

Saulo tortured himself as his mind raced. *What are they doing in the Dominican Republic? Who are they? What's the connection? Is Damani truly in love with this guy? Why would she want to be with that guy anyway? Look at me and then look at him - I have way more to offer her! Why would she want to be with a guy like him? What does he have that I don't? Well let's put him to a real test. I'll find out what he is all about.* Saulo decided to conduct his own investigation and confront Erick.

In their hotel, Zack had finished packing and stopped by Erick's room. He knocked on the door, and yelled through, "You ready?"

"Yeah, I'm just waiting on Damani to come out of the bathroom." Erick threw his bag over his shoulder, gathered the last of his things out of the hotel room, and yelled back through the door, "Give me 10 minutes and I'll be down to the front desk to check out."

As Zack's footsteps trailed away, the bathroom door opened and Damani ran out, ripped off her clothes, and pulled Erick's pants down.

"Damani, I have to go."

Now on her knees, she looked up at Erick, "Papi I wanted to give you something to think about on your way home."

"Damani, Oh my god, stop, I mean don't stop... shit, damn that feels good... baby, I really have to go, we are going to miss our flight."

"Is it so bad that you spend one more day? Aren't you going to miss all of this?"

She continued to pleasure him, and then a knock rang out from the door once again.

Boom! Boom!

"E, yo we got to go!" Zack said with urgency from the other side of the door.

"Okay, Okay, I'm coming." Erick chuckled, then thought, *I mean, I will be!*

He picked Damani up from her knees, threw her face down on the bed, and climbed behind her. As he slid inside her, he thought, *I'm going to rabbit fuck the shit out of you then!*

"Okay. Good. Good." Damani looked back at Erick as he smiled. A tear rolled down her right cheek. Erick wiped it with his hand and gave her a kiss on the lips. "Damani Baby, I really have to go."

They both fix themselves up and headed out the door. The driver, who had been outside waiting for twenty minutes, looked at his watch in disgust. Erick and Zack apologized for running late and hopped in the van. To their surprise, Damani hopped in too.

"Where do you think you are going? You are making this really hard to leave you. Driver do you mind dropping her off at work. She said it is on the way."

Zack looked at Erick holding up his wrist pointing to an imaginary watch "Come on man, really?" he said.

Erick, Zack and Damani said their last goodbyes, and then she hopped back out the van. As the van pulled off and down the street, Damani stood in the middle of the street waving goodbye. "I love you Papi! I love you too Zackary! Come back and visit soon," she yelled.

Erick looked at Zack, "Do we really have to go?" He stymied a fake cry. "I just don't want to leave her and this beautiful country."

Zack burst out laughing. "You a damn fool. Yep times up, but we can always come back soon."

"Let's plan the next trip as soon as we get back to the States." Erick suggested.

"Bet that!"

The van ride to the airport was a quite short one. Erick and Zack hopped out the van at the airport and made their way to the ticket counter to start the check-in process.

Smoothly, Zack reminded Erick, "Hey don't forget to fill out those custom forms."

Zack went through the metal detectors, handed his documents to security, grabbed his bags from the security scanners, and headed towards customs.

Erick walked through the metal detector, handed security his identification and boarding pass as instructed, and collected his bags from the security scanners. Before he could lift the bag to his left shoulder, he felt a hand on his right one. The security agent looked at him, then to the ID in his hand, then back at Erick.

He held his hand up, motioned for Erick to wait, and then mumbled incoherently into his walkie-talkie. A voice quickly responded back, but Erick still remained at a loss as to the situation.

The security agent asked Erick his name.

Erick responded accordingly, "Erick."

The agent looked at his paperwork again and Erick's ID once again. "Sir please pick up your bags."

Wow that was strange, Erick thought. He started to lift his bag to his shoulder, and then was once again greeted by the agent's hand on his shoulder.

"Please wait right here." Ten minutes passed and Erick was still standing there, in the same spot, waiting as he was told when Zack walked up.

"What's going on? I've been waiting for you before I get into the customs line."

"I have no idea. I have nothing on me. All I know is he looked at some paper, my ID, and then me, and told me to wait here. It's not like I went off when I went through the metal detector or they were on alert to anything in my bag."

The agent returned and approached Zack. "Hey you! You must move on. No waiting in this area!"

"You going to be okay?" asked Zack. His face reflected both bewilderment and worry.

"Yeah I don't have anything on me and I didn't do anything. Go through customs and I will meet you on the other side by the departing gate. I have no idea why they are stopping me. It's probably one of those random checks like we have in the States. No big deal."

Ten more minutes passed by and Erick was still standing there; waiting.

"Please have a seat over here," the agent said as he returned.

Erick failed to maintain his normal, calm, demeanor. Agitated, he asked, "What the hell is going on? I demand to talk with someone. Where is your supervisor? Let me know what's going on and why you are holding me here. I don't have anything on me, nor did you find anything in my bag. You are going to make me miss my flight."

"Please sir, I understand. Just be patient and sit quietly. The agent in charge is on his way." A few minutes passed. "Okay sir, here comes the man in charge. Please grab your bag and they will be taking you to the back room."

"For real y'all can check me right here," Erick dropped his bag on the floor and held his hands up in the air. "Again I didn't beep when I walked through the metal detector and there is nothing illegal in my bags," Erick barked to the agent.

"Mr. Erick."

"Yes that is me."

"My name is Special Agent Rodriquez. Can you please follow me?"

"Okay man, whatever, where are you taking me?"

"I will explain everything to you once we get back to the interrogation screening room." Although highly agitated, and against his will, Erick reluctantly followed Agent Rodriguez.

"We are stopping you because you fit a profile description. We have had a problem with drug trafficking lately." Rodriquez explained.

A description huh? More like profiling. Erick thought to himself. Erick looked at him and laughed nervously.

"Believe me sir, this is no laughing matter."

"Look man," he said as he now pointed at the original security office that stopped him, "I already told this guy that I don't have anything on me."

Agent Rodriquez continued to loudly, his voice now louder than Erick's. "Fine, will you agree to a body search?"

"A what? Body search? For what?" Erick said offended and shocked at the request.

"Your refusal shows just cause to hold you further." Rodriquez said with impunity.

"Fine dude. Do what you got to do. I don't have shit on me." Erick said defeated and now fuming.

After Erick agreed, the first agent performed a true "jail-style" pat down.

"Please remove all items out of your pockets. Please take off your shoes and socks. Please remove your trousers. Please remove your shirt. Please open your mouth and stick out your tongue. Please hold your hands in the air and slowly turn around."

"See I told your ass! NOTHING! What do you want me to do now, bend over and cough" Erick said smartly.

"Okay sir, please get dressed. This paper says that you gave your consent to be search, such search was performed and the results came out to be negative. After you sign this paper we will take you directly to your plane as it is now boarding. Thank you and we are sorry for the inconvenience."

"Yo E, I thought you weren't going to make it. What happened?" Zack inquired.

"Man, they did a full body search for drug trafficking."

"Ha! Ha! Your ass always is fitting some description and somebody's profile. Your ass can't even take a nice vacation without being harassed by the cops." Zack said as he lightheartedly poked and teased at the trauma that Erick had just endured.

"That shit ain't funny Zack. They had me hemmed up in some back interrogation room. Whatever must be making it through this airport must be serious."

They both burst out laughing.

Erick regained his normal composure, "Well, ain't this another story for the books! Well, back to the crib for the daily grind and bullshit!"

CHAPTER 11

UNDER INVESTIGATION

There is nothing worse than sitting at your desk at work daydreaming about beautiful women, sandy beaches and blue water, Erick thought.

The first couple of weeks after returning home from vacation left Erick feeling amazing. He was on a high, refocused, and with boundless amounts of energy; especially after feeling he had met the woman of his dreams. Erick and Damani talked at least once a day and had huge phone bills to prove it. Erick eventually changed his cell phone plan to accommodate how much they actually talked.

Thank god for international calling plans and calling cards! He sighed. *What we have is real. I think I'm starting to believe in all those fairy tales about love at first sight.*

"Hey Papi when are you coming back to see me? I miss you." Damani asked this frequently. In fact, Erick had started to keep a ledger with tally marks in it. He glanced down, pulled it from the desk, and made a quick guess at the total. *Yeah, that's gotta be at least 100.*

After a few months, the phone calls became less frequent. Inevitably, when they did happen, the subject always turned towards his return trip back to the DR. On one of those calls, Erick promised Damani that he would be coming back to see her in a couple of months.

"There are a few things here that I need to take care of before I can come back over to the Dominican Republic. I mean, my schedule is pretty flexible, but I still have responsibilities." Erick tried to explain.

Erick noticed that Damani started acting a little different, distant, and less affectionate when she talked to him on the phone. He could tell that she really didn't believe that he was coming back for her. Perhaps it was the calls he missed, or the times he couldn't talk long because he was in the middle of something. Erick tried to convince her to just give him a little time. The less frequently they talked, the more Erick's insecurities started to doubt her loyalty.

Did she find a new man? Who knows this could be a game that she plays with new men she meets all the time. She says that she got a new job with more responsibilities that keep her extremely busy.

"Have you heard from her?" Zack asked.

"No not really? Last time I talked to her she said she had a new job and was really busy. Well, you know it was fun while it lasted, but I don't have time for her to make up her mind if she wants to be with me or not. Really, was I supposed to move to the DR or get her to the States somehow? I mean, I hope she is alright. You know she got mad at me over some B.S."

"So while I try to get in touch with her, she has been saying she is working; Even all hours of the night. I don't mind, I have my own life to live and things going on here at home. I can't keep worrying about what she is doing all the time. I have to trust her and she has to trust me."

He then thought to himself, *when we get to go back I will see her then. I even bet that we fall right back into the love thing we first felt for one another.*

He turned his attention back to Zack and his previous train of thought. "Matter of fact I think, I might surprise her and not even tell her I'm coming in town until we are already there. I know you are in, but I will send out an email to the other fellas that didn't get to go with us the first time to see if they want to hit an all-inclusive resort for a few days in Cabarete, and then later in the week we can have the driver take us so we can see Damani and friends in Puerto Plata."

"Sounds like a plan to me. Let's get this trip booked as soon as possible so I have something to look forward too." Zack suggested.

Back in DR, the task force had been deep undercover, following members of the family, plotting out their routes of money pick ups, and they even witnessed one store owner getting beaten. Through their investigation, the task force had built an extensive list of suspects, filling their wall, but also found themselves unable to identify all of them. Only a few key players within the Cruz Family had been identified. El Commodore was still the primary target, labeled the "main shot caller"; the one responsible for giving all the orders.

Although a part of the Cruz Family, Damani was eliminated as a suspect on the "Wall of Key Players" as she was deemed unfit of doing such tasks as trafficking and murder. There was no evidence linking her to any criminal activity, and their perception of Damani as a woman, no more, no less, blinded them to her strength.

Damani often thought of Erick and living the "American Dream," but realized that she could never leave her family in the DR.

It would be nice if we could live happily ever after here in Dominican Republic, she would often think to herself; a smile gracing her face momentarily. *Pablo already offered Erick a job all he would have to do is accept the offer and move here.*

She knew in her heart that just as it would be impossible for her to leave the DR, it would be equally hard for him to leave the States.

But hey, a girl can dream.

In moments of clarity, when dreams didn't cloud her reality, she knew if Erick moved, she confessed to herself that she would have to explain any legal and illegal activities to him for his safety and the family's secrecy.

What he did not see or know of her past was advantageous to her. Her father was growing old and had been ill a lot recently, and Damani had assumed a vital new role within the family business. After a long discussion with her father about a new way of doing things, he gave her his blessing, but insisted she prove herself before he would grant her full control. All decisions were still his to be decided in their finality.

Her goals, unlike her fathers', were to move the family out of the drug and extortion racket and into more enterprising, legitimate, and legal businesses.

She had been reconsidering the old way of conducting business, and knew, that sooner or later, a lot of people were going to end up six feet under, or behind a set of steel bars.

She was skeptical of Saulo and the reasons he offered for his frequent visits, especially since she knew the history between their two families. She also noticed around the time that Saulo moved into the area, unfamiliar faces began showing up around town. Her suspicions were just that; suspicions, but something within her knew that things had changed. Saulo had changed. The town had changed, and she needed to be cautious.

Saulo often insisted on being at the house even though his mother was working and did not have time to spend with him. More than once, he was found wandering about the property by security. He continued to ask Damani out. She admired his persistence, but grew annoyed by the same token. She refused to give any inkling that she was going to break, and consistently told him she wasn't interested and involved.

One day Saulo said, "Oh so you are seeing the American guy? What does he have that I don't have?"

How did he know about him? I never introduced those two together. She quickly dismissed the thoughts as she had more pressing matters to attend to.

With Damani at the helm for a few months, the business had grown and everybody in the family was happy. She decided that the family would purchase a local hotel. It had a restaurant, bar and lounge, and would be useful to launder some of their dirty money.

Damani insisted they hire girls off the streets and employ them as bartenders, waitresses, "exclusive companions" and excursion-tour hostesses. She did, however, continue to offer protection services to several of the small businesses in town.

Why give that free money away? This way the family continued to run the town and no imposters would dare try to come take over. If they did, they would get a huge surprise like Rocco.

Every now and again, she would get a call about some business that needed her special attention. Her uncles' knew these calls should be reserved for only the most special of occasions. She kept a low profile, and made sure that her name could not be linked to any criminal activity. Even though she was the new "shot caller," not a soul *living* in the town knew her name in any respect other than a great businesswoman. Her arrival and departure from said events were handled with the upmost discretion as she was not in the business of getting her hands dirty any longer.

Damani also invested money into a coffee business that Pablo ran. Although their business in the past was strictly an "export" business, a front to get their drugs out of the country, now the family money had allowed Pablo to expand his business, sell more coffee internationally and become one of the major brands of coffee on the international market.

Damani also hid money by investing in different schools and local sports teams. The family now had interests in teams in three different sports; basketball, soccer and baseball.

She devoted her time and energy to fix up old schools, their fields and run down gyms, and for the towns her teams practiced and played in. In return, she received three huge grants from the local government which help hide most of the illegal money they would earn throughout the year.

On game day, the stadium also made a few 100,000 pesos. For those in the neighborhood, she kept the prices low so more people would attend each event. At the end of each season, the Cruz family sponsored a huge block party filled with activities for the children, lavish buffets, live music, and Brugal Rum and Presidente beer at a steady flow. Damani was no stranger to these events, and was often seen playing with the kids and handing out food.

With Damani in charge, crime was down and the townspeople were appreciative for all the Cruz family did in the neighborhood.

CHAPTER 12

CASINO

Erick and his three friends, Zack, Sean and Andrew, walked into the Cabarete Casino after enjoying their day relaxing at the resort. Nightfall found the four dressed fresh and feeling like a million bucks. The sounds of slot machines rang out, people were screaming with joy and frustration, and cigar smoke filled the air. The casino was packed full of people trying their luck. As they looked around, there were a lot of beautiful women working there, as well as "working" there.

"Let's have some fun, play a few games and have a few drinks since we have a few hours to kill before the club starts popping. Who knows we might get lucky." Erick suggested.

It was his birthday, and he was ready to party. As they walked in the door, they were each given $20 in chips to play a game. They were led to a private table game called the group later named *Fuck It!*

The old guy, the "dealer," and his beautiful assistant explained how the game was played to the foursome.

"Place 5 balls in a cup and throw them on this moving spindle with numbers 1-10. After all the balls land, you count up the number of balls coincided on the table. The object is to get 100 total points or four of a kind of each. Nothing hurts you if you can make the bet each round."

"There are ways to win money while playing while you are trying to get to the 100 points. 100 points pays big."

The group exchanged glances, shrugged, and Erick took the lead to play first. He rolled the dice, scored large numbers, looked on the board, and he had just hit for 50 points and 200 in chips for a $20 free roll.

"Remember, I said you need 100 points total," the old guy reminded.

"So let's keep going. I'm halfway there." Erick played on. Usually Erick does pretty well with keeping his bad habits under control, but today, Erick's was feeling a certain type of way. After all, it was his birthday and he felt lady luck was on his side. He shrugged and thought, *I should really cut my losses now and go party with the fellas, but I am so close. Fuck it, let's play on.*

On the next roll, Erick doubled the bet line number, but as long as he can cover the money convert out of the 100 points pot, he would be okay. Three more rolls, and Erick is a 1000 bet line and 80 points.

"Fuck it! At this points let's keep going! 20 more points. The way it's being going, I'm feeling good!" Erick felt he would be fine.

Erick rolled the ball again. Next two rolls, and he had doubled the line 2 more times. Now the line bet was at 3000, but Erick had also gotten to 90 points.

Two more rolls later, and he had scored 99 points.

Fuck it! 6000 bet line to win 100 grand. They can have that money out of my winnings once I get to 100 points! Erick thought to himself.

"Okay, two more rolls. I need 1 point."

The Casino manager had been alerted, and he sauntered over to the table, and quietly watched the action and Erick.

As Erick is about to roll, and win a huge payout, the casino manager tells Erick if he reaches 10,000 on the bet line then Erick would need to cash out and then resume playing.

"No problem, 10,000 pesos… cool that's nothing. Zack what is the conversion rate on 10,000 pesos?"

Zack, being the math wizard he is, quickly came up with a $240 estimate.

"Ok, No problem," Erick laughs. "I think I can handle that."

The old man then speaks up, "Son, this game is not in Pesos it is U.S. Dollars."

"Dollars? American? WHAT THE FUCK? Did you just say $10,000 AMERICAN DOLLARS? Did he just say 10 stacks American?" Erick felt like he was going to faint and puke, but wasn't sure which one was more imminent. Zack, Sean and Andrew stood there with their mouths wide open in disbelief of the situation at hand. Their lively demeanor shifted as if they were now pall bearers at Erick's soon-to-be funeral.

Erick took a deep breath. "Okay, I'm at 6,000 and 99 points. I Need 1 point to win 100 grand. FUCK IT!"

On the exterior, Erick tried to be flippant and present a carefree attitude, but on the inside his stomach churned, his palms began to sweat profusely, and he knew didn't have $10,000; not even $6000 American.

Erick decided he has to try and get this one point before he reached the $10,000 mark that meant he would have to cash out. He gripped the cup, rolled, and the balls hit the board.

The dealer totaled them up. "No winner. What do you want to do?"

Erick was sick to his stomach but put on a brave face. "I'll keep going and bet again."

The bet line increased another $3000 and Erick was now up to $9,000 bet. *If I don't win on this next roll then I am FUCKED*, Erick told himself. *Either way I have to go for it. One point for 100 grand, and they can take the money out of my winnings for the bet line.*

Erick was already in deep. He closed his eyes and said a little prayer, *if I hit this 100 grand I will pay for everybody's next trip*. With sweat dripping down his brow, he took a sip of his Johnny Walker Black label.

This 100 grand would not only pay off all his debts, but would help finance all his other ventures without having to take bank loans or raise the money.

"1 roll to win!" Erick shook the cup. "1 roll to win." Erick rolled the balls. He closed his eyes. The dealer can be heard counting the numbers up.

"Sorry, missed the point by 1 number."

Erick was stuck on 99 points and had to go cash out. Erick clutched at the invisible knife that seemed to be digging deeper and deeper in his chest.

One damn number! One damn point! Oh this hurts. What are my options? Erick began to plot. *They got all the exits covered. I can't run or they might try and bury me and the homeys in a sugar cane field. Stuck on 99 points!* Erick couldn't get that thought out of his head. *I could have won that game if I had the amount to pay the bet line cash out. So what are my options here? Let's man up and take the loss like a man. That's why it's called GAMBLING!*

Erick was escorted to the back of the casino to the manager's office. The manager ran all his credit cards and took the cash he had won from the game. When the total was given to him, Erick still owed the casino $8,000.

SHIT! Where the fuck can I get $8,000 in the middle of the night? Erick decided to call his cousin. Unfortunately, he was out of the country, Japan, and didn't answer his phone. After thinking about all the consequences of failure of payment; taking a physical beating, cutting off fingers or broken bones to death... Erick came to the only conclusion he could think of.

I'm going to have to bitch up and call my damn momma! Shit! He took a breath and rehearsed what he was going to say as he dialed the number.

"Hello?" Erick could tell she was sleeping from the sound of her voice.

"Hey mom!"

"Hey Erick."

"Look before you start yelling, I'm okay, but I made a mistake and I don't need you to yell at me right now. I need a favor." Erick took a deep breath and said, "I need you wire to me $10,000."

"YOU NEED ME TO DO WHAT?"

"Yes Ma'am, I need you to wire me $10,000."

Erick assured her upon his return to America he would pay her money back in full. She reluctantly conceded to wire the money the following morning when the bank opened, but Erick knew he owed her big.

After the phone call with his mother ended, Erick told the casino manager that the additional money owed to the casino would not be available until the next day. "There is nothing I can do right now or she can do, the banks are closed," he said somewhat apologetic and begging for mercy. The thoughts of losing fingers or being buried in a sugar cane field ran quickly through his mind.

"Erick, it looks like you need a drink." The casino manager pulled out a bottle of Johnny Walker Blue from his desk drawer and told him to help himself. As Erick took a few shots, the manager took down all of Erick's information and explained what was going to happen next.

"I need you to be back at the casino at 9 a.m. The driver will be there waiting for you at the resort at 8:30 a.m. Great, I will see you tomorrow so we can get this balance taken care of first thing. Hey," he said patting Erick on the shoulder, "these things happen. You win some, you lose some. Keep the bottle."

Erick was banned from the casino for the remainder of the night, but they left his game open with a line of credit for him for after the wire came through.

In hindsight, Erick thought, *I should have taken the chance and played the next two rolls. One out of three odds to land one point for $100,000?*

The group decided that the night couldn't end there; after all it was Erick's birthday. He tried to feign as if he was unphased by what had just transpired, and walked out of the manager's office with his bravest face. He found the rest of the group waiting for him out in the Casino lobby.

"Hey y'all ready to go? Everything has been taken care of." Erick lied to his friends. "We are on vacation in Cabarete, Dominican Republic... Now let's go have a great night and continue to celebrate my birthday."

Erick and the fellas went to party it up - VIP Style! Erick paid the casino/club that night – and suggested the least they could do is comp him drinks and a section in the club. That's what they did. The $10,000 had not been a total loss.

Slowly, Erick relaxed and the thought of losing almost $10,000 seemed funny. It helped to have three friends there with him to tell him how crazy and stupid he was, and they also told him how glad they were that he was the one who lost it.

Erick joked with Zack, "You know, it was one of those fuck-it fuck-ups. I couldn't really explain where the outcome was going to be; really bad or really, really good."

The casino manager was happy Erick stopped playing because they didn't want to pay out $100,000 American Dollars. The casino manager told Erick that he was the first person to get to that amount of money.

Erick thought, *I bet they are taking that damn game out of the casino after I leave!*

Erick and his friends were treated like Rock stars that night; bottles of liquor, music, dancing, and lots and lots of women.

The next morning at 8:30 a.m. on the dot as promised, the limo driver was outside waiting for Erick. Still hung over from the night before, Erick peeked inside the blackout limo just to make sure he wasn't being set up.

Okay, cool. It's empty.

The limo drove out to the Advanced Check-Cashing Money Bank center in the middle of the rough part of town. Erick noticed as he stepped out of the car that there appeared to be only one way in and one way out of the building. There was brick barrier wall with bobbed wire strung along the top. Erick wondered if that was to keep people in or to keep people out.

The driver told Erick to walk down to the end of outdoor courtyard and the door would be on the left at the end of the building. The driver watched Erick as he walked down the courtyard and as he reached the door got back in the limo. The courtyard looked like something out of a horror movie. The majorities of the stores were empty and boarded up. One store looked like it had suffered major fire damage. There was no plant life other than the weeds pushing through cracks in the concrete.

Erick reached the end of the courtyard where an armed guard stood outside a bullet proof door and in the window a small sign read *Banco*. "Guess this is the place" Erick joked. The guard didn't seem amused at all and rang the buzzer on the door. Before the door was opened a password was given by the guard to be let in the door.

Once Erick walked through the outside door, there was another locked glass door. The casino manager opened the door. "Hello Mr. Erick, glad you were able to make it, on time, and we didn't have to come looking for you. Please have a seat"

The casino manager pulled a seat up to the desk where one lady was counting money. There was another older lady sitting at another desk working on the computer, and behind them was what appeared to be a bulletproof one-way window, the kind that are at the police stations when they conduct criminal line ups and don't want the accuser to be seen by the criminal. The door leading to that room had a key code lock on it as well.

As Erick took a seat, his phone rang and it was his mother.

"Hello?"

"Hello, are you okay? What is going on Erick? You have me worried sick?"

"Mom, I'm fine. I am sitting at the bank. I will explain everything to you later. Was the transfer made?" He dared not to tell her what kind of place he was really sitting in. Erick had to calm her nerves.

"Didn't I tell you I would make the wire transfer? I had to do all this running around this morning to try and get the money transferred from one account to the other, and then the bank manager said they will make the transfer to your account. The lady at the bank said the transfer was made at 10 a.m. and the money should be in the account, but no telling what time it would be in there."

"Ok, so in a few hours; Great mom. Thank you very much, and again I will pay you back when I get home."

"I know you will bye." *Click.* Erick's mom hung up the phone, and he knew he was going to hear about this in more detail at a later date.

As Erick hung up the phone, he told the casino manager that the transfer had been made. Erick tried to explain to them how American banks work, but knew it would take a little time before the money reached the account. The casino manager picked up the phone to make a call to his boss to explain the situation.

Damani picked up the phone. "Hello?"

"The counts were off last night," says the casino manager, "that Negro Americano lost $8,000 in the casino and couldn't pay the full amount last night and could there be an extension made for him."

Damani yelled loudly, "Get my money by any means necessary. If you don't get the money by noon then I will personally come down and deal with it. I usually don't make it a point to make examples out of Americans, but this day for $8,000 I will have two unmarked graves in the sugar field. Now get the money!"

"No La Jefa I will take care of it. No need for you to get involved."

"You better or the American would no longer have the only problem" she yelled. "You have until noon."

After the phone call with his boss, the casino manager dropped his friendly act, and became more aggressive. No longer was he kind and understanding, but instead seemed determined and firm. "I need this money by 12 noon. Call your mother back," he urged.

"No. I am not calling her back. For what? Why? She said she made the transfer and we are just going to have to wait. I told you it takes time. You just heard the conversation I had with my mom. She said the money will be in my account before noon. And quit trying to run my cards until the money gets there."

The casino manager had the lady at the desk run Erick's credit cards two more times, like he was hiding additional money from them, and this pissed Erick off. He stood up and began screaming at them. Now standing face to face with the manager with his chest poked out.

"I told you quit trying to run my fucking cards! The money is on its way! What you gonna do? Shit! Nothing! You kill me, hurt me? NO MONEY! We both have to sit and wait, like I told you the last three fuckin' times. The money is on its way dumbass."

Erick quickly calmed down after he noticed the little lady counting the money at the next desk placed a small caliber pistol on the table from beneath her desk.

Now if the little old Lady pulling heat, I damn sure don't want to find out who or what is behind that tinted one way glass - watching all of this. For all I knew they could have a gun on me right now. Shit nobody knows where I am. I ain't about to get popped and I know the money is on the way. Erick thought to himself.

Erick kept a straight face the entire time, and never wavered in his composure. He told the casino manager and the old bitch with the gun, "I see your guns. Frankly, I am more afraid of what's going to happen when I get home with my mom than anything you can do to me."

He knew that probably wasn't the right thing to say, but at least they knew he wasn't scared. Inside, however, Erick was worried, *oh my god, oh my god, oh my god!*

Erick didn't have a clue to where he was, nor did his friends. His mom had his cell number for them to track, but they could easily toss that. Erick tried to figure out where he was, and determined he was only about twenty minutes down the road from the casino in a gated project.

"Okay, Okay, let's both calm down. Since we have about an hour to waste, rather than sit here, let's go have a drink and get something to eat." The casino manager suggested.

Erick and the casino manger walked down to the opposite end of the courtyard and got a bite to eat at a small nearly empty restaurant. Everywhere Erick looked were gates with barbed wire and nowhere to get in or out.

Damn where am I? All I know is that this grilled ham and cheese is not about to be my last meal damn it. Erick was really hoping that the money got there soon. He bummed a cigarette from the waitress, sat and drank his beer and said a little prayer to himself. *Just let the money be in the account when we get back so I can get away from these people. I am tired of them and I know they are damn sure tired of me.*

"It's going on noon, let's head back. Hopefully for both our sakes the money is in the account," said the casino manager.

Finally, after refreshing the computer several times, the money was in the account. Erick called his mom and thanked her for making the transaction. He quickly hung up. Short conversations provided less details, and Erick was in no mood to divulge too much in front of this group. Erick just wanted to pay that money, hop back in the limo, and leave. *They can't withdraw that money fast enough!*

At 11:45 a.m., Damani started gearing up to take the ride to the bank where the Americano and the casino manager were. Her phone rang, and on the other end was the casino manager.

"Everything is now paid La Jefa. No need for you to come down. I apologize for the mistake on my part. It won't happen again."

"Let the American go! That's the last thing we need is for one of them to come up missing again. You remember what happen last time? Confirm all the debts are paid, take your cut and drive the American back to hotel resort like nothing happened."

When the manager placed the phone back in its place, his hand stretched out for a handshake. Erick felt a sense of relief, and made a joke or two about seeing him next time he was in the Dominican Republic. He quickly made his way back to the limousine and headed back to the hotel.

As Erick walked back into the resort, the fellas were walking down to have lunch. He kept his morning activities to himself, content to keep what happened, and what could have been, all to himself.

CHAPTER 13

CONSPIRACY THEORIES

"Dos cervezas y Dos Tequila, gracias por favor". Erick ordered two beers and two shots of Tequila from the waitress for him and Zack. "Can I also have the arroz con pollo? Zack what are you getting to eat?"

"For you sir?" Asked the waitress of Zack.

"I'll have the ribs and fries, gracias."

"Hey where are Sean and Andrew?"

"I got a text from Andrew saying he was going to relax by the pool and meet up with us later, and who knows where Sean is. He is probably with that chick he met the other night...knowing him."

"Speaking of chicks, E how was your night with Damani?"

"Honestly Zack it was kind of weird. She treated me like I was a whore. The only thing she didn't do is leave the money on the dresser". Erick said jokingly.

Zack erupted in laughter.

"After we got back from the club, I got a phone call saying she was on her way. She came over about 3:30 a.m., got her some dick, and then she fell asleep. I know I have been known to knock 'em out, but damn. It was nothing like before. About 9 a.m. she got a phone call and she threw on her clothes and was quickly out the door. When I asked her where she was going she said she had gotten called into work. Maybe she just wanted to see me while she could, knowing that she was going to be busy the entire time we were here this trip. It's not like I gave her a heads up we were coming to town."

"Damn no morning quickie and cuddle time? Aw you miss her!" Zack said teasingly.

"Shut up Zack! Seemed like a pattern to me. Even when I would call her from the States she was kind of short with me. She would say 'Papi my boss wants me to go on this run' or 'I have to take care of the books for my job'. She has been acting really funny lately almost like she was hiding something."

"I wonder what that is all about?" Zack said with concern.

"You think she got another man visiting her when I'm not here? You think she has a Dominican Boyfriend?"

"Naw, can't be. What would she tell him when she stays out all hours of the night with you? The first time y'all met she practically was with you the entire vacation."

"Now I definitely wouldn't put anything past her as far as being sneaky. She is always on the phone. When she talks to me in Spanish she talks slow but you ever notice when she doesn't want us to know what her and her girls are talking about they start talking really fast".

"Yeah I noticed that too." Zack agrees.

"Yo, but she does that all the time with me. What she doesn't realize is that I'm starting to pick up on what she's talking about. For example, one day her and Candy were talking about a guy, and I said in English 'what about this guy named Saulo? I'm your only boyfriend.' They both had a crazy look on their face like 'I can't believe he understood what we were talking about.'"

"Zack, have you noticed that she knows everyone? The kids all know her and always run up to her. The old ladies vendors always just give her candy off their carts. I usually give them a couple of bucks for it just to be nice, but they never ask."

"I noticed she knows everyone, but I just figured that was because she grew up here. The town is only so big," Zack says.

"All the women that are here won't talk to me when she is around, or as soon as they find out that I am with her, they give me a crazy look and walk away. But they always hug and say hello to her. Remember that's how we got close to begin with. The first day we met, me and Yosi were sitting at the bar and I was getting crazy harassed. All of a sudden she came and the women stopped flocking. I started calling her my little protector. Then when you came she would bring you girls to meet. She knows all the girls."

Erick continued with his observations, and Zack seemed to be tracing his mind for glimpses of truth in them. "You ever wonder how we always got a seat at that bar, table at the packed restaurant, didn't stand in the line at the club, nor do I even remember paying? Zack think about it. She introduced us to her 'friends;' the military police on the corner. She said 'this is Erick and Zack,' like she was saying to watch out for us. She always introduced me as her man. You notice that? Even at the bar, the fine bartender wouldn't flirt with me after she found out who I was waiting for. I believed she even apologized to her."

"Yeah I did see that." Zack said.

"Do you ever notice that nobody harasses us anymore like they did when we first started coming here? It seems like after that first trip everything changed. What was the common factor in all of this? Yes, Damani. Even though I met Yosi first, he would continue to always look after us. I swear Damani knew when we come in town each time too."

"Yeah she got eyes on you brother. That Dominican phone must have a tracker in it when it touches back to DR… it pages her." Zack says jokingly

Erick laughs. "Shut up Zackary. That's not funny."

"Ha Ha when your ass goes through customs, the officer has a special Erick button he pushes that alerts her Iphone." Zack now laughed hysterically

"You're an Idiot Z! Come to think about it, doesn't her cousin or friend work the front desk of the hotel. He is probably watching us too. You ever notice how security never asks for ID when I take her back to the hotel and she can come and go as she pleases?"

"Ha! Ha! That's because her family probably owns it. Shit, they probably own the whole town. You have been dating the Boss's daughter. We already started calling her little boss. Now what if she was actually the Boss? Or connected somehow? Like what if she was like a King pin? Like when they show on TV those big busts. She could have been the Queen Pin chick, and have millions of dollars and guns and shit all in the crib." Zack dreamed of conspiracy theory after conspiracy theory.

"That would be crazy right?" Erick sat idly, intrigued by Zack's theory.

Zack continued, "What if she was like a queen pin killer chick. Like when she went off to the bathroom she was dealing drugs, or making big deals. What if every time she said she had some business to take care she was killing people? It already seems like all the women are afraid of her for some reason."

"Yep it's weird, the guys respect her, and the ladies fear her. Us together, nobody says anything. Even when it's just me and you Zack, it's like the word got out…don't fuck with those two right there or you are going to have to deal with the boss. Novio la Jefa y Amigo [The Boss's Boyfriend and Friend]," says Erick.

"Well E, if she was some type of boss, wouldn't she have some protection? She always walks around with no protection."

"I guess if you know everyone in town and they respect your rep then what they going to do? Erick suggested.

"How about my girl Candy? What roll does she play?" Zack questioned.

"Okay…Candy? Let me think." Erick paused. "What if she was like her female body guard. You see how Candy was ready to put a bottle to the girl's neck at the afterhours spot for trying to talk to you."

"Man I was drunk. I forgot all about that." He admitted.

"For real E, in the short time we have been visiting here, think about all the people we have met, the pool parties, brunch at the mansions with her friends, the VIP tables at the clubs, and free drinks. We even got job offers to stay here in the DR. You ever think any of this was out of the ordinary?" Zack questioned.

"No not really? I don't feel like I am ordinary peoples."

"Ha! Ha! Ha! Alright John Legend! You got jokes."

"Shit, he made that song just for me. That's my theme music." Erick sang out loudly, "I'm not ordinary peoples…"

Zack busted out laughing. "Erick you stoopid!"

"Dude, now what if she was really heavy into shit? You would think the FBI or whatever…the DR FBI would be hip. You can't run an entire city and nobody notice. The rich are rich and the poor are poor. Somebody got to get paid off. Shit, she did know all the cops, and not to mention those were military cops she introduced us to too. Who knows who else she knows; politicians, lawyers, judges?" Erick continued the conspiracy theory diatribe.

Zack added to it, unable to stop himself from embellishing, "Now the DR FBI got her under radar looking into the corruption in the city. That would be insane."

"Okay, so now think Z, every time someone came up to us, what if they were undercover? The ones she shooed away like she didn't know? What if she knew they were feds watching us? Remember how she wouldn't let us take certain taxis? We could only get them from her friends and taxi companies."

"E, have you ever noticed or wondered why she always sits with her back to the street? What if they were taking pictures or had her and her family under surveillance somehow? Man, what if we were under surveillance just because we know her?"

"Yeah that's weird Zack, because most people don't like sitting with their back to things because they want to see things coming. Okay, I got one… so what if getting stopped at the airport wasn't just a coincidence either?

"Was it a coincidence the second time it happened in DR? And the one time in Miami? Oh yeah, I forgot. Erick you had just fit a description. They had your picture on a wanted poster. I'm going to stop going places with your ass."

Erick laughed. "Shut up Zackary, you love me…. We in this together for life! You would be bored if you tried to travel with anyone else." Erick held up his glass towards Zack's, "Roadies for life! CHEERS! Besides Z, you are the only one that knows where I keep my bail money!"

"Good the food is here, let's eat!"

———

The clock on the wall now reads 12 noon. The TV in the background is blaring, and a voice erupts with official business:

"Rompiendo News- interrumpir la programación regular con noticias de última hora historia- Un gran golpe se ha tratado a la Cruz del cartel. Más detalles por venir después de esta pausa commercial."

["Breaking news - We interrupt the regularly scheduled program with a breaking news story. A major blow has been dealt to the Cruz Cartel. More details to come after this commercial break."]

CHAPTER 14

THE RAID

A rooster crows in the distance in the little town of Cabarete. Saulo looked at his wristwatch. 7 *a.m.* He surveyed the room. He watched as the team members loaded their weapons, and readied equipment for the day's task. *Doomsday*, he thought.

Unlike the rest of the team, Saulo had already been fully dressed in his tactical combat gear for three hours. He stood in the front of the room, cleared his throat, and attempted to motivate his team. "Attention! Attention everyone!"

"Over the past two months we have gathered enough evidence through our undercover efforts to start bringing these criminals to justice. Today we will deal a devastating blow to the La Familia Cruz Cartel. We have been granted the DR SWAT Force to assist us in our cause. We would like to welcome them. They will watch our backs, and we will watch theirs. Today will be a challenge for all of us. Do not take the Cruz Cartel lightly. If given the opportunity, they will fight back. They need to be taken by surprise. We must move swiftly so they cannot warn one another."

"We have four teams. We will start from the bottom of the board and work our way up the list until we get "El Commodore" Esteban Cruz. For clarification purposes, that means we take out the two Lieutenants and the Captain first. At 9 a.m., we will hit the first three houses at the same time. Once those houses are secure, I will lead Team 4 in the capture of 'El Commodore.'"

"My team, and my team only, will be responsible for "El Commodore" and we will make sure we hit him last as he is the biggest threat. It is extremely important that we take them out fast, quietly, and do it today. No mistakes can be made. If they slip through our fingers then it will be that much more difficult to catch them again. The last thing we need is the Cruz family to remain in business. They are extremely dangerous and have been terrorizing the Northern Dominican Republic neighborhoods for years with their drug trafficking and extortion tactics. Our goal is to cut the head off the snake and the body will fall."

"There is no shame. We are doing God's work. Kill them or arrest them; it doesn't matter to me. We are taking back our towns one by one. By noon, I want reports all over the news of a successful operation. We will be successful today and reach our goal, or we will die trying."

Saulo bowed his head and said a quick prayer. "Bless us oh lord, even though we are small in number, may we strike like a mighty army driving the crime, corruption, and enemy out of our midst. Let us be victorious. Amen."

The teams synchronized watches, and set all radios to frequency 19; the secure line of the Task Force.

"Does everyone understand their assigned orders for today? If not, speak up and we can go over them again. We have to get this right today people. Again no mistakes!" Saulo reassured himself that everything was set for a successful operation.

"If there is nothing else "Now let's go get some! Load up!"

The task force and swat teams loaded into unmarked cars and vans, and headed towards the assigned sting locations.

———

It was now 9 a.m., and Agent Rodriguez checked the status of his teams. "Is everyone in position? Team 1 Check in. Team 2 Check in. Team 3 Check in."

"Team 1 here. Everyone is in position."

"Team 2 reporting. In position."

"Team 3 is a go!"

"Team 4 is also in position. We are holding our position down the street from the Cruz Compound. We will be waiting on your reports. Maintain radio silence for the next 30 minutes until after you breached to premises." Agent Rodriguez ordered.

———

At 9:01 a.m., Team 1 approached the 1st Lieutenant's house. A male member picked the lock to the house and the team entered. They cleared the first few rooms and found the lieutenant in his boxers, talking on the phone, and making breakfast in a small kitchen.

"Policia! Jorge Hernandez, put your hands up and stand still. Is there anyone else in the house?" The leader of Team leader yelled. "Go check the rest of the house and make sure that we don't have any surprise visitors." He ordered.

Startled by the intrusion, Jorge immediately hung up on the call he was on and placed his hands in the air.

Cell phone in hand, still holding his hands up in the air, Jorge re-opened his phone and hit speed dial number 2 on his phone. A tired "Hello" answered on the other end. "Code Red" he yelled, and threw his phone down, smashing it to pieces. His actions startled the cops holding him at gunpoint and they opened fire, hitting him with a barrage of bullets.

"Agent Rodriquez, Suspect 1 has been terminated" Team 1 leader reported.

———

In another part of town, Team 2 made their way through a beautiful rose garden at 9:01 a.m. They found an open window used for air-conditioning the room, crawled up and over, and reassembled inside the 2nd Lieutenant's house. Once in the room, they divided into two smaller teams, half made their way through a narrow hallway and up the stairs to the second story of the house, and the remaining group cleared the bottom level. The upstairs team reached the master bedroom with guns drawn. "Freeze, Policia! Papo Hernandez, Don't Move," they yelled at the bodies lying motionless in the bed. No movement was made from under the covers.

The leader pulled back the covers and revealed pillows arranged in the shape of a body. As he looked down towards the foot of the bed, he discovered to his surprise… a bomb with a digital display which quickly counted down. Two minutes…1:59…1:58..

As he ripped back the covers on the bed, he had also released the pin that triggered the bombs countdown to detonation.

"BOMB… everybody out. It's a trap. Less than two minutes. RUN!!!!"

Frantic, the upstairs team struggled to make it through the doorway as they collided with one another. The first man down the stairs reiterated the leader's words, "BOMB, Run! Run!"

The last few members didn't make it out the front door, but instead dove through the glass windows. As the last person was being pulled to safety, the house blew up. There were only minor injuries suffered from diving out the windows and getting hit with debris. Somehow, everyone made it out alive, but just barely.

"The house was booby trapped and no suspects were inside. We made sure to clear each room. Once we reached the bedroom we found a bomb." the team leader reported to Agent Rodriquez.

Saulo was pissed but there was nothing he could do about it right then and there.

Target 3 was Capitan Luis Vega's house. At precisely 9:01, Team 3 breached the front door and cleared the bottom level of the house. They hugged the stairwell wall, and heard noises from the upstairs bedroom. As they made their way up the stairs, they could hear several voices coming from a room on the right. The team swung the door open, and in bed was the Capitan, naked, and two naked women.

As they raised their guns, and shouted "Policia," one of the women screamed and jumped from the bed. She lunged toward the first officer through the door, but he smacked her with his gun and knocked her to the floor.

The second female rolled on her side, pulled a drawer in the night-stand open, and began to turn with a large revolver in hand. Before she could completely turn towards the team, she was riddled with 12 bullets in her back and head. The gun fell from her limps hands and made a thud on the floor next to the unconscious woman.

With all of the commotion caused by the women, the officers had been momentarily preoccupied. In the melee, Luis had fled to the next room, down a set of hidden steps, and out the back door of the house. To his surprise, as he reached the back lawn, he was immediately surrounded by the DR Swat team. Standing there in all of his glory with guns drawn on him, he knew he was caught.

"Luis Vega, Put your hands in the air! Get down on your knees!... Lie face down on the ground." Barked Team 3 leader over a bull horn. "Go put the cuffs on that naked fool and somebody please find him some clothes."

The naked Capitan was cuffed, picked up off the ground, and was placed in the back of the dark van.

"Agent Rodriquez, Team 3 has suspect 3 in custody."

———

In Erick's hotel room, the sun is beaming through the shades. Damani's phone rings, and she hesitates to pick it up.

"What time is it?" Erick questioned.

Damani's phone displays 9:01 a.m. As she got up from the bed, and answered, she uttered a tired "Hello."

The person on the other end of the line yells "Code RED," and the line went silent. *Code Red.... There is trouble*, she said to herself.

"Papi I have to go to work, they are calling me in early." Damani quickly put her clothes on and gathered her things. On her way out the door, Damani began to dial her father to get some information on the emergency.

"Hola Papa, Que Pasa?"

"Hola Damani, Donde Estas?"

"I just left Erick at the hotel and I am on the way to the house."

"No Damani, CODE RED. You know what that means. I have been informed that some special task for is conducting a raid. We are getting hit today and it can be any minute now. You know what you are supposed to do. Do not come here and get caught up in a sting operation. I need you to go to the designated safe house. I have already sent Papo to meet you there. Obey my orders."

"Papa, why didn't you go with them? You still have time to get out. I can come get you. Meet me by the back entrance."

"Damani, I am home lying in my bed. I'm too old and too sick to be running from anyone or anything. How much longer did you really expect me to live? I am tired of pissing and shitting on myself. I am tired of not being able to enjoy life. I do not want you to have to take care of me or see me in so much pain."

"Besides, this is good for the family and the business. We need to make it look like someone is taking a fall... make them think that they are winning or stopping something, so you can continue to run the family when I am gone."

"Over the past years you have proved yourself worthy of being my sole successor and have made me proud just as you did as that little girl all those nights ago in the Slums. Even back then I knew you were strong. I am sorry Damani to even have brought you into this life. I robbed you of your innocence."

"Papa don't talk like that. I asked you."

"I should have been man enough to keep you away. I set such a bad example for you. You could have grown up to be a doctor, lawyer, or anything else. I turned my only daughter into a thug, a killer. Find love Damani, like I once loved your mother Consuela. Have some children and keep the Cruz Family a legitimate one from now on. We have enough money stashed for you to tie up loose ends and walk away."

"Damani, I love you. Do as you are told. I have to go. They are here."

"El Commodore" hung up the phone without Damani getting in another word. He broke open his phone, removed the chip out, and dunked it in a glass of water next to his bed. He propped himself up in the bed and waited for the Agents to reach his bedroom. He closed his eyes and said a little prayer to himself:

"Dios, I know I haven't been the best person in life, but I did it all for my family. You know my heart. Forgive me for my sins and please keep Damani safe and out of harms ways. Thank you. Amen"

As Esteban finished his prayer, his bedroom door swung open.

Damani tried to call her father back but to no avail. She gets a message from the phone company instead: "Lo sentimos, pero el número al que está tratando de llamar no podemos ser alcanzados en este momento."

["We are sorry but the number you are trying to call cannot be reached at this time."]

———

In another van, just down the street from Cruz Compound, Saulo and his team are prepared for their raid.

"Once I hear back from Teams 1-3, we are going in to get "El Commodore." We know every morning that his security detail gathers out back for their morning soccer game. This will be the perfect time to detain them all at one time as they will have their guard down and be unarmed."

"If we surround them we can quickly take them down without bloodshed. "El Commodore" will be left in the house alone. Once we have the security detail in custody, I will then go in and bring "El Commodore" out peacefully. We have a past relationship and he was like a father to me when I was a kid growing up. If anyone is going to bring him out it will be me. He is an old man now and won't put up a fight. Nobody is to come in after me. Is that understood?"

"Now all we have to do is wait for the other Teams to check in."

What seemed like hours has passed, and Saulo checked his watch constantly. There was a flurry of walkie-talkie mumblings, phone calls, and then an ecstatic announcement from Saulo, "well, that's it. All teams have checked in, and we're a go! Let's move in!"

Team 4 quickly moved into their positions onto the compound. On Agent Rodriguez's order, they converged on the back lawn from all angles. The security detail was, as expected, in the middle of their morning soccer game. Upon seeing the Task force and Swat team, they immediately placed their hands on their heads and fell to the ground.

"That was as easy as taking candy from a baby. Pussies didn't even put up a fight. What a security detail! Take them all and place them in the van," Saulo ordered. "I'm going in to get El Commodore."

Saulo reappeared a half-hour later through the front door of the Cruz house. He dragged with him the lifeless body of "El Commodore." He dropped his dead body on the front lawn for all to see.

"Well so much for peacefully. Somebody call the Television news and make sure they get this. Esteban Cruz is no longer with us. El Commodore is dead. The Cruz Cartel has been dealt a major blow today. The head of the snake has been cut off. This has been a successful mission."

All the cops on the scene began to cheer and congratulated Saulo on a job well done as he posed for pictures over El Commodores dead body.

CHAPTER 15
BREAKING NEWS (THE SHOWDOWN)

Saulo entered the Cruz house alone and made his way to El Commodores bedroom. He opened the door with his gun drawn and found Esteban lying in his bed watching Television.

"Hello Saulo. What a surprise. What are you doing here? Are you here to see your mother? What's with the gun?" asked Esteban

Saulo yanked El Commodore out of bed by the arm and onto the floor. He kicked El Commodore in the stomach. "Shut up old man. I know you killed my father."

El Commodore laughed holding his stomach. "Ha! Ha! Ha!... You fool," he laughed as he was on his knees doubled over in pain.

Saulo kicked him again. "You killed my father. Admit it.... Juan Manuel Rodriguez. I know you remember him. You killed him."

"HA! HA!" the old man laughed and spat blood in Saulo's face. "Juan who?"

Saulo wiped the blood from his face; disgusted. "You old asshole."

"You think it was me? Ha! Ha! [Coughs] You got it wrong! That was a long time ago." Esteban smiled as he remembers how Damani sliced Juan's throat and how extremely proud he was of his little girl that day.

Saulo hit Esteban with his gun. "What are you smiling at? Admit it, you killed him. Admit it!"

"Okay, Okay... I didn't kill him but I know who did." Esteban laughed hysterically. He flashbacked to a time when he ran the family with an iron fist, before Damani took over the family, and moved things into a more legitimate environment.

"We are different people now. I are completely legal now. Nothing illegal. I get an allowance of my own money to spend from the advisory board.... Ha! Ha! You got it wrong. We are legit these days. I use to use my land for cocaine, but you know what is more profitable... chocolate and coffee."

Saulo smacked him with the gun again, knocking him down to his knees, and then to the ground.

Fighting to pick himself up off the ground El Commodore made it back to his knees. He continued to fight, "The blood of my family runs strong. You think I have been running the family alone these past couple of years?" He coughed.

"You probably got a big ass board with all our pictures on it and you got me as the head. You can take out my Captain and my Lieutenants but you will never take down the La Familia Cruz. We have built one of the most powerful organizations the Dominican Republic has ever seen. You don't exactly know how big we really are or who our influences reach. Even you can be reached Agent Saulo. You think you are safe?"

"Oh man...I am already dying." The old man spit more blood from his mouth, and grabbed for the barrel of Saulo's gun.

"Fucking Punta, do me the favor. Do me the honor. Make me a Martyr. Do you really think that you are going to take me to jail? Take ME to jail? I will be out next week. Matter of fact, I will be staying at the warden's house as his guest. Send me there. His wife will cook me my meals and his kids will bring me my slippers and cigar. His maid will get on her knees and chupa me pene [suck my dick] as I drink my scotch. Do me the favor. Speaking of maids... isn't your mom..."

Saulo hit him again.

"Ha, you can't shoot me. You're a Special Agent. The government's bitch. You are here doing nothing but taking out of these people's mouths. What they have built in spite of getting nothing from the government. The Cruz family has helped these people. We show them how to get a little in this world, but you have to give a little. You say you are cleaning up, for what? Speaking of cleaning…Now back to that maid… Want me to tell you how good your mother's mouth is; better yet let me tell you about your whore of a sister Gabriella."

Saulo angrily hits Esteban again with his gun. Esteban held his head from the blow and felt the blood as it trickled down his face.

"Let me ask you this Saulo? Why would I have even employed your mother if I killed him? Do you think I would want that reminder around me every day? We kept her employed because we knew she had kids and no husband to rely on anymore. Now if I killed him, would I have employed your mother dummy? You and my daughter once were friends. You didn't know I knew you two would sneak candy and cookies. How she made sure you and your sister had toys to play with."

"How she was devastated when you left and cried for weeks! Your mom sent you away! Not me. I would have groomed you into a fine young man. You're not blood, but could have come and been a part of my family. I always wanted a son. All you would have had to do is prove yourself. Now instead of being a rich man, driving a fancy car, and maybe having a hot woman on your arm like my daughter, instead you beating your feet on this hot ass pavement, a slave to a government…living paycheck to paycheck.

"Look in the nightstand, top drawer, and take the money in there. Take that $100,000 and just walk away, like you didn't even see me back here. We can forget this even happened and I will make sure you get more money later, and your mother is well taken care of for the rest of her life."

"So you are trying to bribe me? You think this is all about money? You think that is going to bring my father back? Do you know what my mother had to go through? Fuck you El Commodore, and you can keep your money."

Saulo waived the gun at El Commodore, and motioned for the old man to kneel at his feet. El Commodore was in pain and struggled to sit upright, but crawled towards him. Saulo grew impatient with the slow moving old man, grabbed the back of his shirt, and forcefully dragged him across the floor. "I said sit your motherfucking ass up right here."

Finally on his knees, El Commodore struggled up enough strength to speak. "Saulo, I have to tell you something. Saulo are you listening?"

"What is it old man?"

"You're a little bitch, just like your bitch ass daddy."

"What did you say about my daddy old man?"

BANG! BANG!

Saulo fired two shots into the chest of El Commodore. Esteban clutched his chest in pain as he slowly keeled over head-first onto the ground.

As he laid on the ground, he looked up at Saulo and said, "You shot me....you fucking shot me. I loved you like a son. I am so sorry that it was your father."

Esteban shook and trembled, and continued to sputter blood, "I am sorry Saulo. Forgive me."

"Forgive this!"

BANG!

One more bullet made its' way through Esteban's body, and this one exited through his right eye socket.

Over the walkie talkie Saulo spoke, "The head of the snake has been cut off. The head of the snake has been cut off. El Commodore is DEAD."

As Saulo dragged El Commodore, bloody and lifeless, from the house, his teamed cheered. The corpse was dropped on the lawn and the three bullet-holes still seeped blood.

Damani tried to call her father back ever since they had spoken, but to no avail. She worried. It had been several hours, and she had heard nothing from him, or anyone in the family. She decided to try and calm her nerves and watched her favorite show, CSI. Twenty minutes into her program, a special report came on the television:

"Breaking News! We interrupt the regularly scheduled program with an urgent news story. We are getting reports that Special agents were involved in an extensive sting operation this morning against one of the major organized crime families in the Northern Dominican Republic. Sources say that the sting ended with major players of the Cruz Cartel being arrested or killed. Among the confirmed dead is the Cruz Cartel's Boss, Esteban Cruz, better known as El Commodore."

"The indictments for those in custody include charges of extortion, loan sharking, conspiracy to commit murder, drug trafficking, prostitution/human trafficking, and money laundering. There are also allegations of political corruption and voter tampering."

"I have here with me the lead agent on the case, Agent Saulo Rodriguez. We understand that you were the one to actually take down Mr. Esteban Cruz. Wasn't the goal to have him standing trial for his crimes?"

"Yes it was. However, under the circumstances, I felt that my life was in danger and I had to take action."

"Can you tell the people how it all went down?"

"As I made my way through the house, I found him watching television in the living room. I announced myself as Special Agent and he reached for a gun and gave me no choice but to take action. It was a good shooting."

"How do you feel?"

Saulo poked out his chest and began to boast and brag "How do you think I feel? Me and my team did a great job today! The head of the snake has been cut off. You see him lying there on the front lawn for all to see. The Cruz family cartel has been decimated. All the key players have been arrested or killed in action. The mission was a successful one. After months of investigation we met our goals of dismantling one of the most powerful organized crime families in Northern Puerto Plata. It's a great day for the good guys! Now that's all I have to say. No more questions!"

"Again that was Special Agent Saulo Rodriguez, the Agent Directly responsible for taking down the Cruz Family Cartel and as he put it, 'cutting the head of the snake off,' by putting down notorious Cartel boss Esteban "El Commodore" Cruz. Now back to your regularly scheduled program."

Damani watched the TV and could not believe her eyes. "My father is dead?"

The longer Saulo spoke, the more furious Damani became. She threw a glass and broke the TV.

"Saulo, you are such a fuckin' liar. I knew you were bitch ass no good cop." Damani screamed at the broken TV. "I had just talked to my father. He was lying in bed sick. He was an old damn man who had no time or strength to reach for a gun. You murdered my fuckin' father in cold blood! You disrespected me and my family by dragging his damn body out of the house onto the front lawn and making a mother fuckin' spectacle and mockery of our name."

"You think, you think just cause you killed my damn father that the Cruz Family dies. You just don't know do you. I run this family! I run this Bitch! You think you know me mother fucker, you don't know me. You test me. I'll show you. You don't test me. You got me fucked up. I'll get you back when you least expect it. You want some of this, some of me."

In rage, she flipped over the desk and threw a chair across the room. "You killed my father. You think I don't know what goes on in my town? Agent Saulo Rodriquez you have crossed the wrong one. You think you can't be touched? Revenge is coming for you! You will feel the wrath of the mother fuckin' La Jefa!"

Damani fell to her knees, crying, and mourning over her father.

Following the shooting, Saulo was placed on administrative leave by Internal Affairs. A standard procedure, but one that allowed him to spend time telling the story of taking out "El Commodore." The two weeks passed quickly as a result, and Saulo has been taking full advantage of his 15 minutes of fame.

Wherever Saulo went, someone asked to hear his story. He had several press interviews for magazines, newspapers and television. There was even a parade and recognition dinner given in his honor. At the dinner, he received the prestigious award for heroism and met the President of the Dominican Republic. With all of his new found fame, he even decided to write a book about his life and how he single-handedly took down El Commodore. Upon his return to the office his colleagues stood and cheered; welcoming back their superstar Agent.

"I got a Package here for Agent Saulo Rodriquez? Saulo Rodriquez? Is there an Agent Rodriquez here?" The courier spoke loudly from the front of the room.

"Here, over here." Saulo poked his head through a group of surrounding colleagues congratulating him on a job well done against the La Cruz Cartel.

Saulo shook the box. "Well it's not ticking." He laughed and his coworkers joined him. "You guys didn't have to get me anything." Anticipating it was a congratulatory gift from his colleagues, he ripped open the package as he prepared a speech in his head. Saulo removed the newspaper packaging in the box to reveal three smaller objects.

There was a small card and two small velvet-covered boxes. He pulled out the card and set it aside in a rush to get to what he thought might be the real presents. Like a kid on Christmas morning, Saulo smiled and shook the small velvet box.

"It's not too heavy, too light to be a watch...was it a metal of some kind?" He opened the first velvet-covered box. No, it wasn't a watch but a Rosary. Saulo thought it kind of looked like the one his mother wore. As he showed off the Rosary, he smiled and said, "Thanks, you all know how religious I am."

He held in his excitement as he opened the second box, but closed it quickly before the others could see what was inside.

"Is it that good you don't want to share it with us?" Come on what is it? What did you get? Bet you it was something nice from the Mayor or Governor for doing a job well done."

With a concerned look on his face, Saulo snatched open the card and read it. Deflated, he immediately sat down at his desk and placed his hands on his head. He scurried to open the box with the rosary and inspected it further.

"Well what else did you get" all of his colleagues asked?

Saulo couldn't answer them. One of his colleagues snatched the box from his desk and opened the box for the rest of the colleagues to see. Upon viewing Saulo's "gift," one of his colleagues threw up in the waste basket, another shrieked in pure horror, while others sat mute. The colleague who now held the box became confused by the reaction of the others. He slowly turned the box around, and saw a woman's bloody middle finger. Startled, he quickly threw the box down on the desk in front of Saulo.

Saulo sat in shock. He continually turned the rosary in his hand, whimpered quietly to himself, and stared down at the card, which contained a handwritten message:

> *Agent Saulo Rodriguez,*
> *Vengeance will be mine.*
> *La Jefa.*